# PROTECTOR IN A KILT

## KILTED HEARTS
BOOK 4

## KAIT NOLAN

TAKE THE LEAP PUBLISHING

# 1

"Mom! It's her! It's her!"

The whisper shout carried across the hotel lobby. Well used to being recognized, Isobel knew she should keep walking. That was what she'd been trained to do. Not to interact with the public, except under controlled circumstances. But a quick glance to the left, behind her dark glasses, showed her a child of maybe ten, standing with his mother. The boy clutched a violin case in his hands as he stared at Isobel with wide-eyed excitement.

Feeling the weight of her own instrument case in her hand, she wavered. She was early for their scheduled departure to the venue. Her keeper hadn't made it downstairs yet. Saying hello to a fan wouldn't hurt anything.

Switching directions, she strode over, shoving her sunglasses to the top of her head and offering a warm smile. "Hello."

The kid lost a couple of shades of color from his cheeks, blue eyes going even wider as he blindly tapped at his mother's arm. "You're... You're Elizabeth Duncan."

*To the rest of the world, anyway.*

But she didn't drop the smile. "I am. And what's your name?"

"T...Tobias."

"It's nice to meet you." She nodded to the case still clutched in one white-knuckled hand. "Do you play?"

Tobias nodded like a bobblehead doll.

His mother wrapped an arm around his shoulders. "For a couple of years now."

"That's wonderful. I've been playing since I was little, too." Isobel remembered what it was like when music was new, when she'd been able to play simply for the joy of it, and she envied the child.

Apparently emboldened by the interaction, Tobias took a step forward. "You're my favorite musician! I have all your albums on my phone!"

Warmed by his enthusiasm, she dialed up the smile. "Thank you. I'm flattered. Are you in town for a competition?"

"Uh-huh."

"Are you nervous?"

He hugged the case a little tighter. "Yeah."

Isobel remembered those days, too. She crouched down to the boy's level and dropped her voice. "Can I tell you a secret?"

He leaned closer. "What?"

"I get nervous, too."

"You do?"

"Sure do. Know how I beat it?"

"How?"

"All those butterflies and ick that you feel when you're nervous about something are the same physical responses in your body as excitement. So you can kind of reprogram that message in your brain by telling yourself that you're excited. And once you pick up the instrument and start to play, you lose yourself. Everybody else doesn't matter."

"Wow!"

Enjoying the conversation and feeling a little reckless, she made a snap decision. "You wanna try it?"

"How?"

Isobel knelt and opened her own violin case. "Play with me."

Tobias's eyes went big as saucers. "Really? Now?"

"I have a few minutes. What's your competition piece?"

"'Han Solo and the Princess' from *The Empire Strikes Back.*'"

Grinning, she lifted her instrument. "I approve. C'mon."

The boy scrambled to pull his own violin from the case, and they checked their tuning. She'd already drawn the bow across the strings when she felt the shift in the air, that frisson of cold that told her she'd miscalculated, and her time was up. But she was in it now. A crowd was already beginning to circle around them. Her manager would do nothing in front of prying eyes or rolling cameras, so she'd finish this out and wring every drop of pleasure from the encounter.

Isobel let herself sink into the music, glorying in the synergy that came with playing with someone who held true talent. The boy was good. Not as good as she was at his age, but few people were. By the end of the song, every single person in the massive lobby had stopped to listen. Multiple phones were held up, recording. As applause echoed through the space, Isobel lowered her violin and beamed at Tobias. "Take a bow."

Pink all the way to the tips of his ears, he clumsily folded himself at the waist beside her.

At the edge of the crowd, Paul was waiting in his bespoke suit, his face an even mask. But she could see the storm beneath. He didn't have to say a word.

Quickly returning her violin to its case, she straightened. "I have to go. But it was really nice to meet you. Both of you."

Tobias's mother beamed. "Thank you. You've just made his decade."

"Good luck with your competition.'

The boy waved. "Thank you!"

As soon as she was within arm's reach, Paul's hand settled on the small of her back. Isobel's skin crawled at the touch, but she moved toward the exit so as not to cause a scene. She'd been well-trained not to do that, either.

The car was waiting. The moment they were inside, Paul addressed the driver. "We're late. Make up some time."

"Yes, Mr. Burgette."

As they pulled out of the hotel drive and into the flow of London traffic, Paul raised the privacy screen, locking them into relative isolation. "You're playing a sold-out concert tonight. What the hell do you think you were doing?"

The furious whip of his voice drained away the joy she'd taken in playing just to play. She sank into the seat, as if that would give her any extra space from him. "Just having a little fun with a fan."

"Fun? You don't get paid to have fun. You get paid to work."

The truth was, she barely got paid at all because the revenue she generated through concerts and album sales went to accounts to which he held the purse strings. She was granted a small stipend. An allowance. Because he took care of everything else. That had been the pattern of their relationship since he'd signed her as a client at just twelve years old.

"It was one song. It didn't hurt anything."

"You don't waste your talent on the unpaying masses."

Of course not. Because in his world, nothing was free. Including her. She was a product, not a person.

"It's my talent to spend where I choose." The words slipped free, fueled by a deep-seated resentment.

Paul's hand snaked out, fingers closing around her wrist in a grip so hard she could feel the bones rub together. She barely held in the yelp and wince as he leaned into her space. "Your talent belongs to me. Your music. Your performances. I own you."

As it was true, she didn't argue the point. Trembling, she murmured, "You're hurting me."

He released her, breath coming fast.

Isobel ran careful fingers over the tender flesh of her wrist. This wasn't the first time he'd man-handled her, but he'd never left marks before. Gently flexing the joint, she knew she'd have to ice it or she'd never make it all the way through her performance. She'd been skating dangerously close to this edge for a long time, testing the boundaries of her prison. It seemed today she'd gone too far.

It wasn't like him to be careless with her. To risk her ability to perform. To leave marks where anyone could see. He was escalating, and that scared the shit out of her. She knew what he was capable of when challenged. The threat of it had kept her in this cage more effectively than any lock.

Knowing her only move now was placation, she attempted to salvage the situation. "Dennis told me it's good optics to interact with fans." She picked one of the execs at her record label, knowing Paul wouldn't do anything to jeopardize the contract that had made him a rich man.

He sighed, his tone softening in the Jekyll and Hyde switch at which he was so adept. "Elizabeth, your job is to make the music. Mine is to worry about everything else. Including fan relations. You know we're on a very tight schedule. Courtesy of your little free concert, we're going to be late for soundcheck, and it'll throw everything else off. Do you know how many people are waiting on you?"

As if she were some sort of diva making unreasonable demands instead of spending ten minutes with a fan? But Isobel felt the familiar weight of guilt settle over her. There were dozens of people who'd be at the venue. Lighting and sound technicians. Roadies. Security. Not to mention all the additional musicians who were part of her show. All those livelihoods depended on her doing her job.

Keeping her gaze downcast, she gave him what he wanted. "I'm sorry, Paul. It won't happen again."

"No. It won't." The finality in his tone warned her that the already short leash he kept her on was about to be tightened to a chokehold.

Her stomach curdled at the idea of her world shrinking that much more. Things would get worse before they got better. She knew first-hand they could always get worse.

The intercom buzzed. "We're a mile out, Mr. Burgette."

Eyes on the passing streets of London, Isobel took in the signs. A pub. A clothier. A coffeeshop and internet cafe. Some sort of tourist shop with the Union Jack motif screaming from the window displays of every product it could be printed or pasted on. These were places she was never allowed to venture because they weren't part of Paul's plan, and he'd effectively cut her off from making any friends who might have enjoyed such frivolity.

They arrived at the venue, and Isobel schooled her features, knowing all eyes would be on her until the soundcheck was over. She understood her role here and played it well.

As Paul had predicted, everyone was waiting. More guilt trickled through her at that, and she made quiet apologies, hurrying to the stage. She blessed her years of experience for allowing her to smile and nod and give the appropriate feedback when asked, even though her mind wasn't on it. She usually found solace in holding her instrument and coaxing out the music that was both her passion and her prison. But she felt the ache in her wrist where he'd gripped her and knew it was now or never.

She needed to get out. Needed to run. And it needed to be soon, before Paul did more than leave some bruises.

With an odd sense of calm, Isobel made it through the rest of the soundcheck, going through the motions, looking for an opportunity. It came when she spotted Paul walking off with the venue manager. She'd met the other man last night and knew he could talk the ears off a donkey.

Flagging down Paul's assistant, Veronica, she let some of the exhaustion show. "Hey, I'm going to go catch a nap in my dressing room before tonight. Will you see that I'm not disturbed until it's time to get ready?"

"Of course. Hair and makeup will arrive at six."

That would give her two hours. "I'll be ready."

She didn't let herself hurry. That would draw attention. People were everywhere, going about the business of preparing for the show later that night. There was security, but that was on the venue, not directly on her. Once she'd closed herself into her dressing room, she locked the door and emptied her purse, carefully working her fingers into the hole in the lining to retrieve the stash of cash she'd been secreting away for months. She counted the bills. It was only a few thousand pounds. Not a small amount, but a paltry sum to fund an escape.

It had to be enough.

She'd make it enough.

Keeping a few bills out, she returned the money to her hiding place and repacked her purse, taking only those things she deemed necessary, which didn't include the mobile phone loaded with spyware that told Paul every little thing she did. There was little to nothing she wanted from this life. Knowing her long, honey blonde hair would be memorable, she twisted it into a knot to hide its length. She wished she had a change of clothes, but she'd have to make do.

Urgency beat in her blood. Now that she'd made the decision, every cell in her body screamed at her to flee. When it came time to slip out of the dressing room, she hesitated only briefly, staring at her violin case where it rested on the counter. The idea of leaving it felt like amputating a part of herself. It was the last piece she had of her father. But she had a concert tonight. People would notice if she left carrying it and would remember. No one, especially Paul, would ever imagine she'd leave it behind. That would hopefully buy her more time.

Swallowing down the tears, she stepped out into the hall.

No one took special notice of her as she wove her way through the labyrinthine corridors to one of the exits. At least, not until she made to leave.

A security guard raised his brows. "Help you?"

Fighting to keep her breathing even, she smiled and hoped it didn't look as fake as it felt. "You can, actually. I heard there was an excellent kebab shop in the neighborhood, and I thought I'd nip out to grab one before the show. Do you happen to know where it is?"

There was staff to run such errands, but evidently the man was either used to the eccentricities of the talent or really loved his kebabs. "Course I do. You want Kebabish. You're gonna go out this door to the left. At the end of the alley, you'll take a right, and go about two blocks. You can't miss it."

"Thank you!"

He opened the door for her. "The lamb shawarma is brilliant."

"I'll definitely have to try it." She stepped outside. "Back in a bit!"

Forcing herself not to hurry, she followed the alley to the street, in case he was watching. Then she turned in the opposite direction and hurried back the way they'd driven to the venue. Her heart thundered with every step as she scanned the signs. Spotting the souvenir shop, she slipped inside, quickly purchasing a Union Jack baseball cap and a t-shirt with a profile drawing of the late Queen Elizabeth. A block farther down, she found her intended destination. A half-dozen people were scattered through the internet cafe, everyone intent on their screens.

Isobel purchased an hour's time from a bored clerk behind the counter near the door, then made her way to the bathroom to change into the t-shirt and hat. The more like a tourist she looked, the better. As she stripped off the long-sleeved blouse she'd been wearing, she noted the bruises already coming up on her wrist. Those were noticeable, too, but there was no help for it. She just hoped no one asked questions.

Settling in at a station in the back, Isobel followed the instructions and logged in. And at last she had the opportunity to browse without restriction. This was the piece of her escape she'd never been able to orchestrate before: transportation.

A quick search pulled up several websites dedicated to used cars. She clicked the first one and scrolled through, finding few options that fit within her meager budget, none of which had an automatic transmission. Chewing her bottom lip, she moved to the next and repeated the search with similar results. The third site produced more options and had a chat function to allow messaging with the seller. She sent an interested query to every one she could afford and waited, watching her time tick down. Without a phone, she had no way to call any of them, and who knew how long it would take any of these people to respond?

With six minutes left on the timer, a reply popped up.

Isobel leapt, saying she wanted to purchase the car and asking if the seller was able to meet this afternoon.

*To finally sell this thing, I'll meet you right now.*

That didn't bode particularly well for the vehicle, but desperate times.

*I'll take it. Where can I meet you?*

EWAN MCBRIDE EYED the storm clouds building on the horizon above the endless stretch of empty hills. Riggs Moor was one of the most remote places in Britain, which was exactly why they'd chosen it. No cell service. No people. Hell, the nearest public access road was two-and-a-half miles from the trailhead, and they were well beyond that. It was a good place to face demons.

Ewan had conquered most of his, but his friends were still working on it.

Beside him, Finley Patterson unsnapped the chest and waist straps of his pack and slipped it off, leaning it against a rock. He stretched, loosing an enormous sigh as he took in the view. "Damn, I needed this."

"Which part?" Alex Conroy wanted to know. "Us or being well the fuck away from civilization for two weeks?"

"Both. It's harder than I thought it'd be, going back into the real world. How do you make it look so bloody easy, McBride?"

Following his friend's example, Ewan shrugged off his own pack and dug out some electrolyte chews and water. "It's no' easy. I've just been at it longer than you." Some days, those four years since he'd left the military felt like forever. His life now was a world away from his former career as a Royal Marine. He'd followed all the advice, done all the things he'd been advised to do to properly integrate back into so-called normal life. But after all the things he'd seen and done in the line of duty, he'd never feel fully a part of civilian life. That was why he needed these trips with his brothers in arms. They were who he felt most himself with. They were each others' touchstones.

Patterson sucked down water. "Do you actually like running a pub?"

The Stag's Head had been an impulse buy when Ewan had returned to Glenlaig. The place had been part of the village for more than a century. Old John Drummond had run it for decades before Ewan had been born. When he'd died, his kids, who'd long since moved away and built lives elsewhere, had put the business up for sale. They'd wanted to wash their hands of it and had given Ewan a good price.

"It's fine. It's no' demanding work. Nobody's trying to shoot at me. I'm no' having to do anything hard or difficult, and there's value in that because it's given me time to process all the shite we saw and did. It gives me a function in the community. They seem to appreciate it. And it's nice being close to family. My parents and sister are there. My cousins, too."

"But the people." Patterson shuddered. "Sometimes I see these wankers getting all bent out of shape over things that dinna matter, and I just want to bash their faces in."

"Aye, that's hard," Ewan agreed. "But every day gets a little easier. It helps that I actually like where I'm from. At least, insofar as I like anybody. Though I will admit, it's no' as good as hanging out with you lot."

Conroy pressed a hand to his chest. "I'm touched by your sincerity."

Ewan grinned. "You ken you're my favorite arseholes, aye? Even if it isnae quite the same without Quinn." Callum Quinn, the last of their quartet, hadn't yet finished with his military service.

Patterson clapped them both on the shoulder. "He'll get there, eventually. I did."

"Aye, but I'm worried, if he disnae make the call himself soon, a mission's going to make it for him. His head wasnae in a great place the last time we spoke." And that had been a few months.

"We'll be there for him either way. At the moment, I'm glad I like you lot, as it looks like we're about to be trapped together in tiny spaces for a while. That storm's looking mean."

Ewan returned his gaze to the boiling clouds. "I was just thinking that. Disnae look like the sort that's going to blow through quickly."

A roll of thunder underscored the point.

Patterson shrugged. "We willnae melt. God knows, we rode out worse while we were deployed."

Conroy grimaced. "Aye, but now we dinna have to. Frankly,

the idea of sleeping in the wet—which surely we would if that storm's got the kind of teeth I expect—is no' my idea of a good time."

"Civilian life has made you soft, mate," Patterson scoffed.

"Maybe, but I have to second his unpopular opinion," Ewan put in. "There's no proper cover out here. Nothing to stop the wind. It's a two-hour hike back to our vehicles. I say we head back to them and drive until we find a pub. Get a hot meal and check out the weather report. Then make a decision what we want to do next."

Patterson made a few more insults to their manhood before giving up the argument and shrugging his pack back on. "Fine. But you arseholes are buying the first round."

With one more glance at the boiling clouds, Ewan tugged the rain cover over his pack and strapped it on again. "I'm thinkin' we'd best pick up the pace. That storm's moving fast."

"I'm for that." Conroy took off at an easy jog, and Ewan fell into step behind, with Patterson bringing up the rear.

They'd already hiked more than eleven miles today, and that after ten days of trekking through other remote woodlands around the country. His muscles ached, but he tuned out the pain, as he'd been trained to do, and concentrated on putting one foot in front of the other. The three of them ran in silence, all scanning the terrain around them for an enemy that wasn't there. It felt strange to be making this trek in formation, but without a rifle in his hand. Yet he had no desire to pick one up again.

The storm rumbled closer, creeping over the hills and covering everything with a premature darkness before letting loose great torrents of water. Ewan was soaked in seconds, as if a great bucket had been dumped over his head. He kept moving, his feet squelching in his boots. By the time their vehicles came into view, his muscles were at the edge of their endurance, and he was pretty sure he'd added several blisters—

not that he'd admit either fact on pain of death. Despite his efforts to remain active, he wasn't in full mission-ready shape anymore.

With no discussion, the three of them loaded their gear and formed a convoy for the drive back to civilization. In the twenty minutes before the next proper village appeared, Ewan's muscles had cooled, and he'd begun to shake, despite the fully cranked heat of his 4x4. No one was out on the high street when they parked. A sensible response to the gale. He considered digging out a set of dry clothes from his pack, but they'd get soaked before he went three feet. The performance fabrics he wore would dry quickly enough once he got out of the rain.

The pub was dim when they stepped inside. His gaze automatically took in the room, thinking they'd do well to paint the walls white to make it seem less like a cave. But he didn't give a damn about the decor once he saw the low fire burning in the grate. He made a beeline for it, weaving through empty tables and chairs.

From behind the bar, an older woman, with graying hair pulled back into a thick braid that hung over one shoulder, called out in a thick Yorkshire accent, "Sit anywhere you like."

Conroy and Patterson brought up the rear, circling up around the fire.

Conroy extended his hands toward the heat and sighed. "Wouldnae have had one of these out on the moors tonight."

"Much as I want to give you shite about that, I willnae lie and say this doesnae feel amazing," Patterson admitted.

The bartender crossed over, menus in hand. "It's filthy out."

Ewan pivoted, putting his back to the flames and willing his clothes to dry. "That it is."

"What can I get you?"

"Coffee to start thawing us out. Then a meal, if your kitchen's still open."

"I'll see that it is. And I'll scare up some towels for the lot of you."

"Much appreciated. Thank you."

She came back with three steaming mugs of black coffee and a stack of towels that had seen better days. But they were dry, which was the only thing that mattered. The three of them began mopping up.

"Have you seen the weather forecast?" Conroy asked the woman.

"I have. Nasty business. This storm's massive. Stretches all the way into Scotland. They say it'll be with us for three whole days."

"Three days? Well, that puts an end to our hill walking and camping plans, gents."

"We could pick a new location," Patterson suggested. "Head on down to Wales."

The voice of reason, Ewan grabbed a menu. "Let's eat before we decide anything else."

Over pints of lager, bowls rich beef and potato stew, and a thick, crusty bread, they discussed their options. In the end, after checking the projected weather, they called it, deciding to go ahead and split, making their respective ways home.

With back-thumping hugs and promises to meet again in a couple months, they set out, with Patterson headed to his temp job as a trail guide in Wales, Conroy back to Manchester and the construction job his brother-in-law had hooked him up with, and Ewan back to Scotland. It was a six-hour drive and already late. He ought to find somewhere to stay the night. But the food had rejuvenated him, and the prospect of sleeping in his own bed was too great to resist. Putting on an eighties rock playlist, he pointed his Land Rover toward home.

He was regretting his life choices nearly five hours later as his eyes burned from the strain of trying to see through the lash of rain that had beaten his vehicle the entire drive. Mother

Nature was having a right tantrum, and he felt as if he were taking the brunt of it. Having lost the storm-dark twilight, he was relegated to the true dark now as he navigated the empty Highland roads. His internal compass was solid, but he'd found himself relying on the GPS more than usual because he couldn't see enough of the landscape to fully determine where he was.

The middle of bloody nowhere. That's where.

There were no more vehicles on the road here than there'd been back in Yorkshire. Because everyone with an ounce of good sense was tucked up warm in bed, riding things out. At least he'd be in his eventually, and no one expected him back at the pub before Monday, so he could sleep in.

Mother Nature threw down more lightning, as if insulted by the mere thought.

Ewan slowed even more from what felt like a glacial pace, not knowing what lay beyond the next bend. What he spotted —improbably—was light. It was aimed upward, with dark slashes breaking the beam. It took his brain a moment to catch up to what he was seeing.

Headlights from a compact car that had been crushed beneath a toppled tree.

## 2

Isobel hunched over the steering wheel of the Mini hatchback that was older than she was, as if those scant inches would somehow make the view through the windscreen clearer. The wipers swiped at the glass, hardly able to keep up with the torrential downpour. Anemic headlights cut only a car's length ahead through the pitch black. She'd been driving for hours, and her body ached from sustained tension.

She'd left London with no real plan and no specific destination in mind. The car certainly hadn't come with built-in GPS, and without her phone, she was driving blind. Instinct had propelled her onto the M1 and urged her north. Her only goal had been to put as much distance between herself and Paul as humanly possible. At this point, she was most certainly lost, knowing only that she'd crossed the border to Scotland a while ago, leaving the main roads and following winding tracks into the Highlands.

By now, her concert time had come and gone. All those people whose livelihoods depended on her doing her job would be impacted by this reckless act. Guilt kept creeping around the edges of her mind, and she consistently shut it out.

For once, she had to think about herself first. This was about escape and possibly literal survival. If Paul got his hands on her now, after she'd walked away hours before a sold-out show, she didn't want to imagine what retribution would look like. Thousands of fans would have been on their way to the venue already. He never would have imagined she'd run, so they wouldn't have made the announcement about cancelation until everyone had already arrived.

What had he told people? Had he tried to save face? Claimed she was ill? Or had he involved the police, contending some sort of foul play? Her mouth went dry at the idea that the police could be looking for her.

If they found her, she could tell her side of the story, but she had little faith they'd believe her. She had no proof. Nothing but her word. And experience had shown her that was worth very little. Paul was charming and excelled at twisting the truth just so to support his version of things. He'd no doubt convince the authorities she was having some sort of mental breakdown and that he'd tried to stop her for her own good. Hell, he'd spent years gaslighting her, trying to convince her that everything he'd done since her mom had died was for in her best interest. Just like he'd convinced her mom to sign the contract that essentially signed over her life.

Isobel was his golden goose, and he'd done and would do anything to keep her. Who had been on the receiving end of his wrath? Was someone else paying the price for her deception? He wasn't above punishing others for what he viewed as her misdeeds.

She slammed the door on that line of speculation. For years, Paul had kept her in line by constantly bringing up the consequences others would face for her behavior. She'd never wanted anyone else to feel the sting of his mercurial temper, so she'd bowed to his control. So often and so far that she'd nearly broken. He'd conditioned her to take ownership of his behavior. But that was bullshit. In her stronger moments, she knew that. It was those moments that had allowed her to conceive of leaving at all. But she wished she'd made a more thorough plan.

Yes, she'd escaped. But for how long? Getting away had felt like such a huge, insurmountable thing that she hadn't considered what came after.

She needed somewhere to go to ground. A place to hide and figure everything out. At this point, she'd settle for somewhere to simply rest for a few hours. But at this time of night, nothing would be open. She hadn't seen a town or even another vehicle in an hour. There was nothing but this lonely stretch of road, winding through the mountains, and the storm seemed to getting worse.

*Maybe I should turn around.*

Even as she thought it, lightning flashed, striking so close, her vision went white. With a scream, she slammed on the brakes, feeling the tires slip and the car begin to spin. Seconds later, it came to a stop with a bone-jarring crash. Her body whipped forward, head banging against the steering wheel before the airbag deployed—too late—and everything went black.

It was the sound that woke her. A high-pitched whine and a frantic swish-swish she finally recognized as her galloping pulse. Or maybe that was the wipers.

Everything hurt.

That meant she was alive. Right?

Something thumped against the driver's side window, and Isobel jolted back, eyes flying open with a shriek.

A man stood outside the car, torch shining in. For one terrifying moment, she thought Paul had found her. But as the next flash of lightning illuminated the man's face, she registered it wasn't Paul. Big and fierce, this man looked like he was ready for battle. Soaked from the rain, he looked like he'd *done* battle to get to her. Scratches marred his stubbled cheeks.

He was saying something, but her ears were still ringing, and she couldn't make out the words.

The light withdrew, and Isobel blinked again, blearily taking in her surroundings. She was... in a tree? No. A tree had fallen on the car. The bonnet was crumpled, and part of the roof had caved in, narrowly avoiding her head. The windscreen was a spiderweb of cracks.

That was bad.

Squinting, she peered out her window again to see the man doing... something. Was he sawing through a limb? The view was fuzzy. Because of the rain or her eyes, she didn't know.

The driver's side door opened, and she startled again, shrinking back. Had she passed out? That probably wasn't good either. How long had she been unconscious?

The man crouched, blocking the wind and rain with the considerable bulk of his body. "Are you okay?"

She stared at him, taking in the broad shoulders and hard face, addled brain trying to assess whether he was a threat. But though he looked like some kind of warrior, her instincts told her he was a protector, not a predator.

"Can you move? Is anything broken?"

The urgency in his tone made her push through the mental fog to try to answer. She wiggled her fingers and toes. "I... I don't think so?" Her tongue felt heavy in her mouth.

Leaning into the car, he reached toward the seatbelt buckle. "I'm going to get you to a hospital."

No. No, they'd find out who she was at a hospital. Someone would contact Paul, and all of this would have been for naught.

In a panic, she grabbed his wrist. "No hospital."

His gaze searched her face, and his tone was patient. "You have a head injury."

Terror gave her strength, and she squeezed tighter, needing to make him understand. "No hospital. Promise me."

He looked down, and she saw the moment he registered the bruise that had come up livid on her wrist in the clear shape of fingers. Rage darkened his features for a fraction of a second. But not at her. She knew the difference.

His hand covered hers where she still gripped his wrist, a gentle touch at odds with the fierceness of his expression as he met her gaze. "I promise. No hospital."

At his assurance, the last dregs of her energy drained out, and the darkness slid over her again. This time, she didn't fight it.

It was after two in the morning by the time Ewan pulled up to his house several miles from Glenlaig. Rain still streaked his 4x4 windows, though the worst of the storm seemed to have abated. His passenger had been in and out of consciousness on the drive. He didn't like that. Didn't like the idea of not getting her checked out. But he'd promised no hospitals, so for now, he'd get her inside and use his own training in field medicine from the military. He knew enough to assess for the concussion she'd almost certainly sustained in the crash. Maybe once she felt safe, he could convince her to let him call in Doc Albright.

If she stuck around that long.

*First things first.*

He slipped out of the driver's seat and unlocked the door, swinging it wide and flipping on the overhead light before hustling back to the Land Rover. She didn't stir as he opened the passenger door and released the seatbelt, but at least her head had stopped bleeding. The gauze pad he'd taped over the cut was dark with dried blood. He scooped her up and carried her bride-style into the house. Even as a deadweight, she was so damned tiny in his arms. Slim. Fragile.

Abruptly, her body went rigid against his chest, and Ewan knew this time she was truly awake. Her head came up, slow and cautious, and he got his first clear look into eyes that were a starburst of gold, green, and gray. His step faltered for just a moment. Christ, those eyes were a wonder. Old soul eyes.

Then he felt the trembling in her frame and cursed the one who'd hurt her.

"It's all right. You're safe." His voice held more of a bark than he'd intended. Wanting to put her at ease, he settled her on the couch in the living room. "Just rest. I'll get you some water."

When he came back a minute later, with water and first aid supplies, she was sitting up, every muscle tensed as if ready to flee. He set the bottle on the coffee table in front of her and stepped back, lowering himself into the armchair so he hopefully looked less threatening.

"It's a fresh bottle. Seal hasn't been broken." When she only stared at him, he cursed himself for putting the idea into her head that it could've been tampered with. "My name is Ewan McBride. This is my home. You were in an accident tonight. Do you remember?"

If she didn't, promise be damned, he'd be finding her a doctor.

Her cupid's bow mouth pulled down in a frown. "Lightning struck. I spun out. There was a tree." It was the most words she'd spoken, and he heard the faint lilt of Scotland in the quiet rasp of her voice. It was lower and richer than he'd expected.

"Aye. The bloody thing all but crushed your car. You were damned lucky, all things considered." He hesitated. "I need to check you for injuries."

She curled in on herself, cradling her bruised wrist. "No hospitals."

Ewan imagined a half dozen fitting punishments for whoever had put that look on her face, none of which involved anyone ever finding the body. "Aye. I promised. But you didnae walk away unscathed. You've been in and out of consciousness, so I need to check. If it's anything outside what I can handle, I can get the village doctor." Seeing her about to protest, he pushed on. "Here. Away from prying eyes."

"All right." Her voice was a quiet rasp.

Moving slowly, Ewan relocated to the coffee table across from her, setting the supplies aside. He dipped a washcloth into the bowl of warm water and leaned toward her. Those prismatic eyes followed the motion, but she didn't pull back, and he called that a win. Gently, he began to wipe away the dried blood that had seeped free from the bandage. Her eyes widened as she saw the red on the cloth.

"You hit your heid in the crash."

She winced. "Bashed it on the steering wheel, I think."

"You've a bit of a goose egg, but the cut's no' bad." He peeled away the bandage, pleased when the gash didn't start bleeding again. His training meant he could deal with this much quicker than he was, but he had the sense that sudden movements would send her skittering. After more properly cleaning the cut, he dabbed a bit of antibiotic ointment on the wound and some arnica gel on the swelling around it, then covered the whole thing with a fresh bandage.

He held up his hand. "How many fingers?"

"Four."

Folding them down to one, he centered it in front of her face. "Follow my finger."

She did as he asked, her eyes seeming to track the movement without issue.

Slipping out his mobile phone, he switched on the flashlight. "This is going to suck for a minute, but I need to check your pupil reactivity."

She hissed as the light struck her eyes, but both pupils constricted as expected.

"Sorry. Do you know what day it is?"

"Friday, June 8th. Or, I suppose it's Saturday, now."

"Who's the Queen?"

"Elizabeth the second. God rest her soul."

Ewan glanced down at the T-shirt she wore with the Queen's profile and supposed that one was a no-brainer, though blood from her wound spattered the design now. "What's your name?"

She went silent.

He understood this was a matter of her deciding whether to trust him, not an inability to remember, so he merely continued with his exam, asking about the usual concussion symptoms. Headache. Yes. Nausea. A little. Blurred vision. No. Dizziness. No.

"Can you hold out your arms?" He demonstrated, spreading his wide into a T shape.

After a moment, she complied. He had her slowly move each joint, watching for any signs of pain or stiffness that would indicate other injuries. There was some bruising at her shoulder that he presumed crossed her torso, where the seatbelt had dug in, but no signs of breaks or internal bleeding that he could find.

He reached toward her wounded wrist, stopping short of touching her. "May I?"

With another hesitation, she extended the arm.

Her hand was slim and long-fingered, with unexpected calluses. Very gently, he rotated her wrist to get a better look at the bruising. The positioning of the fingers suggested her assailant had been beside her, not opposite. Given her vehement objections to hospitals, Ewan would lay money that she knew her attacker and that this wasn't the first time. He could see the thin tracery of veins beneath her fair skin, and it only reinforced his impression that she was fragile. Physically, anyway. If she'd run from an abuser, there was more strength here than met the eye.

Attention on her wrist, he stroked his fingers lightly over the lines of bone to see if there was any obvious evidence of a break. "Didn't get this in the accident." He only murmured it, wanting to convey that he understood her fear.

"No."

A million-and-one questions popped into his brain. Who put his hands on her and why? Where was she coming from? What exactly was she running from? But he asked none of them, because he could see she was barely holding it together.

Releasing her, Ewan sat back. "Well, you've likely got a concussion, and that wrist disnae seem to be broken. What you need right now is rest. I've a guest room. I'll go make sure there are clean sheets and get you something to sleep in."

He felt the weight of her gaze as he left the room. She was such a little thing. What the hell did he have here that wouldn't swallow her up? After a few minutes of pawing through his dresser, he turned up a T-shirt and some athletic pants. They'd dwarf her, too, but the pants at least had a drawstring she could maybe tie tight enough.

When he came back, she was cuddling one of the sofa cushions, looking lost.

"No one will bother you here." The words slipped out. A reflexive reassurance that probably meant little. She still hadn't decided whether to trust him. He held out the clothes. "Well, except me. I'll be waking you every hour. Concussion protocol."

She accepted the clothes. "Thank you."

Ewan jerked a nod. "C'mon."

He showed her to the guest room across from his. It was Spartan, as most of his house was. His mom and sister had been after him since he moved in to do more with the place. He'd put them off, wanting to take his time. But as he showed his unexpected guest the space, he wished he had more to offer her than this simple bed and straight-backed chair in the corner. "It's no' fancy. It's only me here, and I dinna need much."

"It's a lot more than I expected to have tonight."

Turning, he caught the bloom of embarrassed color in her cheeks. He found himself wanting to fold her into his arms. To soothe the distress in whatever way he could. Feeling his own cheeks heat beneath the two weeks' growth of beard, he took a step back, shoving his hands into his pockets. She was vulnerable, and the last thing she wanted was a fumbling hug from a big brute like him. "There's an extra blanket in the closet, in case you get cold." Because it occurred to him she might not be tall enough to reach it, he pulled it down himself and set it on the foot of the bed. "I'll be across the hall if you need anything."

She nodded.

With nothing left to say, he moved to the door, pausing only to add, "You're safe here."

"Ewan?"

His name on her lips only intensified the desire to shield and protect her. But he turned and met her gaze. "Aye?"

"Isobel Donnchadh."

Her eyes were lit with some sort of resolve. He had no idea whether that was resolve to tell him the truth or stick to a fiction. Right now, it didn't matter. He'd meet her where she was.

"Goodnight, Isobel."

Dipping his head in another nod, he walked out, wondering exactly what the hell he'd gotten himself into.

## 3

Isobel woke to birdsong, in an unfamiliar bed, in an unfamiliar room. Her head throbbed, and her body ached. She started to bolt upright, then hissed as her muscles screamed in protest.

Memories of the night before slammed back to her consciousness. The wreck. Her rescuer. As promised, he'd awakened her several times to ask her questions and make sure her brain wasn't imploding or something.

It definitely wasn't night now. Sun slanted across the wide-planked floors at an angle she thought meant late morning. Easing her way to a sitting position, she peered out the window and saw only forest beyond. No houses. No people. That didn't mean there weren't any. But something about the house felt remote. A world away from cities and tours and Paul. She had no idea where she was, which meant he couldn't possibly know either.

At the idea of that, she took her first real, deep breath in what felt like forever. Ewan had told her she was safe here, and for now, she felt it.

But she couldn't just stay holed up in this room, imposing

on his hospitality. Today she'd have to start figuring out what came after escape. That meant facing him again in the broad light of day.

Her clothes weren't in the chair where she'd left them last night. Flummoxed, she realized she'd have to go out in what she'd slept in. Readjusting the sweatpants, she rolled the waistband over and tied the drawstring as tight as she could. The legs still puddled over her feet. At least she was covered. But it felt weirdly intimate to be wearing his clothes, surrounded by the scent of him. Or at least his laundry detergent. As if they'd shared more last night than first aid.

*Foolishness. What else were you going to put on? He'd hardly want you sleeping on his sheets with bloody clothes.*

Bracing herself, Isobel slipped out of the room. The rich scent of coffee greeted her in the hall, along with the low hum of some machine. A dryer? Maybe Ewan had washed her clothes so she'd have something to wear.

The man himself was in the kitchen, his back to her where he worked at the counter, clad in gray sweatpants and a T-shirt very much like the one she wore. But where the clothes hung on her like a potato sack, they fit him like a second skin, highlighting broad, muscular shoulders and powerful thighs. Tattoos swirled down his arms, flexing as he sliced something, and she found her eyes tracing the lines, trying to identify patterns. He moved with utter confidence and an economy of motion that told her he was very capable. As if the rescue from last night hadn't already made that abundantly clear.

With his wavy dark hair and several days of scruff, this man was about as far as it was possible to get from her world, and she wondered what quirk of fate had led him into her path.

"How's the heid?" His morning-rough voice made her jolt.

She hadn't been as stealthy as she'd imagined.

"A little tender, but okay, all things considered."

"Can you eat?"

A massive growl sounded from her stomach.

"I'll take that as a yes. Sit."

She recognized an order when she heard one, but there were necessities to deal with first. "In just a minute."

Retreating down the hall to the bathroom she'd spotted on her exit, she took care of business before checking her reflection in the mirror. The sight made her grimace. Her hair was a rat's nest, and she looked as battered as she felt. Not much she could do about that for the moment, but she took the time to finger comb the worst of the tangles from her hair and plaited it into a quick braid.

Ewan was sliding plates of food onto the table when she returned. Scrambled eggs. Toast. Fried potatoes. Sausages. "Coffee or tea?"

She preferred tea, but she'd already been such a bother. "Either."

"Coffee's made."

As he poured them both a mug, she glanced around, taking in more of the open living space. It wasn't quite as Spartan as the room where she'd slept, but it definitely hit on the mini-malist end of the scale. A couch and two armchairs flanked a stone fireplace she hadn't noticed last night. Narrow bookcases rose on either side, jam-packed with paperbacks. A few framed photos were scattered about, though she couldn't see any clearly from here. The long rectangle of his kitchen table divided the space, butting up against the back of the sofa, with four chairs tucked in on three sides. A door led off the kitchen, out to the garden, presumably. Beside it, she spotted a boot tray and a set of bowls on the floor.

"Do you have a dog?"

He sat, nudging a steaming mug in her direction. "Aye, I do. He disnae mind particularly well and is incredibly stubborn, so I couldnae really take him on the remote two-week campout I've been on with friends. He's been staying with my sister."

She added that to the picture of him in her head.

"Eat." The word came out gruff. Clearly another order. But there was no meanness or aggression in his tone. He simply seemed unused to having anyone in his space.

They lapsed into silence. She nibbled on toast and sipped at her coffee, watching him plow through half his plate before she was certain her food would stay down. She'd just started in on her eggs when he broached the subject she'd been afraid of.

"Isobel, who put those bruises on you?" He asked it gently. More gently than she'd have imagined for someone who looked like him. Except that she remembered how careful he'd been when he touched her last night, and gooseflesh rose along her arms. Or maybe it was the sound of her name in that deep voice. Her real name. She had no idea what had possessed her to give him that one last night, except that it had felt like the first step in reclaiming herself.

Repressing a shiver, she folded the mug between her hands and tried to figure out what to say.

"I willnae tell anyone you're here. No one even kens I'm home yet. I'm no' supposed to be for another three days. But I need to have some idea who I should be on guard against."

Which suggested he wasn't planning to shoo her out the door as soon as breakfast was through, in which case, it was a reasonable question. Where she went, trouble would eventually follow. Still, her instinct was to be vague.

"My guardian."

His dark brows knit. "How old are you?"

"Twenty-four."

That seemed to surprise him. Because he thought she was too old for such a thing, or because she was older than she appeared without all the makeup and trappings of her public persona?

"You're a grown adult. Why do you have a guardian?"

Okay, probably not the best way to explain.

"It's... complicated. He *used* to be my guardian, and he's having some trouble giving up the role. My mother died when I was still a minor and left me in his care. And that was okay, to start." Paul had been solicitous and avuncular for that first year or two, doing anything necessary to shepherd her through her grief so she could still perform. And she'd done everything he'd said because he was the adult in her life. She'd trusted him to be looking out for her best interests. That was why her mother had signed the contract to begin with, wasn't it? Because she'd been snowed as much as everyone else.

Shaking off the memory, Isobel continued. "But over time, it became very clear that he's controlling and overbearing and doesn't appreciate my attempts to be an adult and make my own decisions."

Blue-grey eyes slid to her wrist and flashed with temper. "Name?"

Of course, a man like him would be enraged by such treatment, and he'd seek to rectify the situation somehow.

If only it were so simple.

Isobel shook her head. She wasn't looking for a white knight or retribution. And she sure as hell didn't want this man to get tangled up with Paul as a result of his kindness.

Ewan let it go. "All right. Do you have a photo so that I know who I'm looking out for?"

"No. I left without my phone. I left without everything. I have nothing but the car, my purse, and what I was wearing."

He winced. "I'm afraid you dinna have the car anymore, either."

She'd been too out of it last night to really register that. "Well, it wasn't much to begin with. Just a way out." The words fell from her lips, revealing more than she'd wanted. She knew better than to reveal weakness.

But, in truth, this man had rescued her from a bad situation. Brought her to his home. He'd had ample opportunity to hurt her, if he was going to. And instead, he'd been nothing but polite, respectful, and kind. She wasn't used to kindness anymore.

Ewan sat with the implied reality of her situation. Isobel wondered what he was thinking. What he'd do.

"Look, I dinna know what your long-term plans are, but I understand that you want to lie low. I can help you do that here."

"Where is here?" She had no idea how long she'd been unconscious last night. He could've taken her almost anywhere.

"Glenlaig, Scotland. It's a small village a couple of hours from Inverness. Only a few thousand people. I can offer you a job and a place to stay, while you get back on your feet, reinvent yourself, or until you decide what you'd rather do instead."

Intrigued despite herself, she sat up. "A job doing what?" She'd never held a normal job in her life, so she didn't have many skills unrelated to music.

"Waitressing. Once your wrist heals. I own a pub. It happens we're short-staffed for the summer. It's no' glorious work, but it's an honest wage. And it'll keep you fed, keep a roof over your head, until you decide otherwise.

She almost laughed because this was so far from the life she came from—a life of incredible privilege where others served her, but she was trapped in a gilded cage. And instead, he was offering her the chance to turn around and serve others in this tiny town that probably nobody had heard of. Certainly no one would be looking for her here.

"What about employment paperwork? Taxes? All that?"

"I can pay you in cash until you're comfortable with something else. I understand the importance of not leaving a paper trail."

He was offering her a safe place to figure out all the After she'd ignored before. It was so much more than she'd expected. Instinct told her she could trust him.

But she'd trusted Paul once, too.

"Can I think about it?"

"Of course."

A buzzer sounded. Ewan rose, crossing to the dryer tucked beneath the counter on the far wall. He pulled out her clothes, bringing them to the table. The trousers were mostly okay, though there were a few dark spots she knew were blood. The shirt, though, was a total loss.

He frowned down at the bloodstained T-shirt. "Hmm. We'll need to get you some clothes."

Isobel tried to think what was left of her nest egg and how far she'd be able to make it stretch.

"There's nowhere much to buy anything in the village, and ordering online will take a few days. Delivery isn't exactly reliable in the Highlands. But I ken where I can borrow some."

What sort of woman did he have in his life he could make such a request of? "And how exactly are you going to explain that?"

"I'll take care of it."

At his simple confidence, a lump of emotion swelled in her throat. This man didn't know her. He was going out of his way to protect her, to make her feel safe, and to give her an option other than continuing to run. Gratitude had tears welling, but she didn't let them fall. She had the sense he was the kind of guy who'd be super uncomfortable with weeping.

Instead, she quickly wiped her eyes. "Thank you."

He cleared his throat and nodded. "You're welcome."

After much consideration, Ewan parked a mile from the village, on an old farm track that wasn't likely to get any traffic, as Duncan Aitkenson's sheep were grazing greener summer pastures just now. He hopped the stone fence and made for the woods. Rather than break cover, he kept to the deep green shadows of the trees as he climbed the hill that led to the stone dance that was Glenlaig's little secret. A thin trail led down from the dance to the alley that ran behind the village high street, including his pub.

It was instinct to wait in the shade, assessing whether he was actually alone, before he hurried to the stairs that led to the flat above The Stag's Head. A little overkill for the situation? Maybe. But years of special forces training were hard to break, and he wanted to avoid questions for now. Better no one know he was back yet.

Moving with the soundless grace that was second nature, he climbed the stairs, automatically avoiding the creaky ones he'd learned in the year he'd lived here before buying his house. If anyone saw him and asked what he was doing, well, he was the landlord. He had a key, and his sister had asked him to check on something.

But no one spotted him before he slipped into the flat. He braced himself for an enthusiastic greeting from his pup, but Havoc wasn't inside. Which meant Ciara had probably broken his edict and taken him with her to work at the pub downstairs so he wouldn't be lonely. Ewan would lay odds he was curled up on a dog bed in the private back room used for parties. He wouldn't complain. It would be easier to get in and out without having to stop and reassure the dog he hadn't been left for good.

His sister's place couldn't have been more different from his own. While smaller than his house, it seemed she had twice as much stuff crammed into it. Color seemed to explode from every surface in the form of pillows and blankets and plants. All those soft, girly touches that made the space feel lived in far more than the minimalist approach he'd taken. He'd never had much reason to give it any thought before. But now he wondered if Isobel felt welcome in his place.

*And what the hell does that matter? She willnae be staying for long.*

Crossing to the bedroom, he moved straight to the closet, quickly pawing through the profusion of garments. Why did anyone need this many fucking clothes? At least she had so many, she wouldn't notice if he nicked a few things to last Isobel until new ones of her own could be acquired. He pegged her as about Ciara's size, but couldn't be sure, as he'd been avoiding looking at her body this morning, because the sight of her in his clothes, with all that golden hair mussed from sleep, had been more appealing and distracting than he'd have imagined. Which was a problem. She was nearly ten years his junior, for Chrissake. Not a child, but definitely not someone looking for... anything. And neither was he. His life now was uncomplicated, and he preferred it stay that way.

But he'd see Isobel safe, first. That was the right thing to do.

He snagged some T-shirts from the bottom of a pile on the shelf, then added some stretchy pants he figured would have a more forgiving fit. Thinking Isobel might get cold, he added a cardigan to his pile. Seeing the small stack, he realized he hadn't thought to bring something to put the clothes in. Getting caught carrying a pile of women's clothes would garner far too many questions and get tongues wagging even faster than his early return. Not finding any sort of bag in the closet, Ewan ducked under the bed to check there for luggage.

The bark was the only warning he got before someone rushed him. Ewan rolled, narrowly avoiding a bat slamming into the bed where he'd just been. As he gained his feet, hands raised in defense, he recognized his sister already preparing for another swing.

"Ciara! Stop!"

She jerked back, letting the bat drop with a thunk. "Ewan? What the hell are you doing?"

Havoc barked again and bounded over, thick tail wagging

hard enough to sweep several knick knacks off a table. Legitimately happy to see his dog and to buy himself some time, Ewan crouched to give Havoc a full-body rubdown. "Who's a good lad?"

"Clearly not you. What were you doing in my closet?" Ciara's eyes narrowed. "Were you playing some kind of prank?"

He sighed and cursed himself, knowing he had to give her something. "No. I was borrowing some of your clothes."

Her dark brows knit at that. "If you've picked up some predilections I'm not aware of, I dinna think my clothes will fit you. And what are you doing back already? We weren't expecting you until Monday."

"Not for me."

Those brows winged up.

If he hadn't been so caught up in thinking about his houseguest, he'd have heard his sister approach. But it was too late now. She'd caught him red-handed. He had to explain, at least a little.

With a speaking glance that told her to stay put, he crossed to shut the door. "I canna give you all the details. I'm helping someone who needs to lie low for a while. She's lost everything, so I need to borrow some clothes."

"She?"

Of course, Ciara would zero in on that.

"Who is this person? Where did you find her? When? Why does she need to lay low? Is she running from something?"

Ewan wouldn't have given her all the details, but the fact that he didn't know the answer to most of those questions himself left him more than a little uncomfortable. He was accustomed to operating on better intel. And he was taking care of that with some help from his brothers-in-arms. They just needed time to get back to him.

"I canna tell you anything more right now. I just need clothes and your silence."

Seeming to understand he was deadly serious, she straightened. "Is this an abusive partner situation?"

"Not exactly that, but a bad situation that she needs to lie low to escape. I dinna have all the details yet myself." Galling to admit, but he was still earning her trust.

"Are you sure she's telling the truth?"

He considered everything Isobel had said. She'd outright refused to give him some details, but he didn't think she was lying. "I ken for certain someone hurt her, and they're not gonna get another chance."

"Okay." Ciara nodded and went into the closet herself to begin pulling clothes and adding them to the pile on the bed. "What color is her hair?"

"What the hell does that matter?"

She waved his bafflement away. "Just... what color is her hair?"

"Blonde."

"What color blonde? Dark or light?"

He growled in irritation. "I dinna ken. No' as light as Connor's." Their cousin was a decent reference point.

"Okay." She pulled a bag from beneath the opposite side of the bed he'd tried and began loading things in. Several outfits. Some pajamas and underthings. Even toiletries. Things he wouldn't necessarily have thought of.

When she'd finished, she handed over the bag. "Here. If there's anything else I can do to help, let me know."

The idea of depending on his sister for anything left Ewan feeling a little flustered, because this was his little sister, the surprise baby who was younger, even, than Isobel, and he'd always been the one to take care of her.

"Thank you."

"You're a good man, Ewan. Whoever she is, she's lucky to have your help."

Flustered by that, too, he turned toward the door. He'd

taken two steps before he spun back. "Listen, dinna let anybody know that I'm back. I want the chance to make sure she feels safe, so I need to avoid people coming out to the house just yet."

"Sure. What about Havoc?"

He eyed his wagging pooch, who was right on his heels. "You're staying here for a little while longer, lad." When the dog whined, he scruffed his ears. "Bring him when I was supposed to be back. Just buy me that much time."

"Consider it done."

## 4

Ewan had told Isobel he'd be gone about an hour and had encouraged her to take advantage of his absence to have a shower and clean up, if she'd be more comfortable that way. As he'd said, "You dinna ken me. You have no reason to trust me. So I'll be sure to stay gone long enough you'll have time to finish. Lock the door behind me."

He wasn't entirely right. No, she didn't know him. But his continued awareness that she'd been through something traumatic, and his efforts to avoid triggering anything or making it worse were a hell of a lot of reason *to* trust him. So she'd followed his advice, lingering under the warm spray until the stiffness began to abate. After, she stood naked in front of the bathroom mirror, taking in the damage from the accident for the first time.

A clear line of bruising crossed from her shoulder down to her hip, where the seatbelt had dug in. There were some abrasions on her arms and face where the airbag had deployed. The cut at her hairline was red, but not angry with infection. Whatever Ewan had dabbed on the area last night seemed to have brought the swelling down. The bruise would be there a while, but it wasn't as bad as it could have been. Her wrist was the worst of it. Visibly swollen, each finger-shaped bruise stood out in stark relief against her pale skin. She traced the dark lines of it, but instead of remembering Paul's threat in the back of that car, she thought of Ewan. Everything about him said rough around the edges, yet he had such a capacity for gentleness. The contrast fascinated her.

In the privacy of his empty house, she could admit to herself that *he* fascinated her. Not that it mattered. She certainly wasn't looking for anything. And it wasn't as if anything would happen. For all his kindness, no doubt, he looked at her and saw someone who was broken.

Deflated by the idea, she turned away from the mirror to dry off and dress in the trousers she'd been wearing yesterday. Despite the fact that it had been washed, she couldn't bring herself to put the bloody shirt back on. Neither did she want to wear the T-shirt she'd slept in. For several minutes, she waffled over whether to go into his room to find something that might fit her better. In the end, she couldn't force herself to cross that boundary into his private space. But she found a button-down shirt in hunter green hanging on the back of the bathroom door, as if he'd gotten it out to wear at some point and forgotten about it. The shirt still fell almost to her knees, but with the sleeves rolled up and belting it tight around her waist, it didn't feel quite so much like she was drowning in fabric.

Nerves skittered. Surely, he wouldn't mind. He'd been so solicitous about everything else. And if he did, well, he was supposed to be coming back with more clothes for her to change into. She wouldn't be wearing his shirt for long.

Needing distraction from her thoughts, she decided to explore a little. On a table by the front door, beside a pile of camping gear he'd presumably brought inside this morning, lay her purse. Had he looked through it? Checked her ID? It wouldn't match the name she'd given him, though that was the name she'd been born with. The name she'd doggedly held onto in her heart, long after it had been legally changed to something easier to spell and recognize by the public.

Carrying the purse to the kitchen, she opened it. Nothing appeared to have been disturbed. But how would she know? Everything would've gotten jostled in the crash. Shrugging off her paranoia, she emptied the bag, counting up what remained of her nest egg. Less than two hundred pounds. Not nothing, but given the car was a total loss, it certainly wasn't enough to keep running. Not without help.

Ewan had offered her that help. A job. A place to stay. A chance.

Really, it was more than that. It was an opportunity to start over. To reinvent herself. She'd been denied the chance to make any kind of choices for herself and her life for years. Perhaps she wouldn't have deliberately sought something humble and working class, but she wasn't too proud to turn her nose up at the offer. Especially as those were the exact reasons Paul would never look for her here. He thought of her as a pampered princess. And maybe there was a little truth to that. The gilded cage he'd kept her in hadn't included a lot of doing for herself. She didn't have normal work experience. But she was no stranger to hard work, and no matter how far outside her comfort zone this situation was, she could learn.

She'd asked if she could think about it, but really, what other alternative did she have? She had to make a living somehow, and it couldn't be with music. Even if it wouldn't risk exposing her hiding place, Paul owned all of it.

Isobel absorbed the fresh stab of grief at the truth of that. Leaving music behind felt like cutting off a limb. But it was too dangerous, so she'd learn to live with it as she'd learned to live with so many other painful things. She'd stay here. For now, anyway.

Wanting to know where here was, exactly, Isobel moved to

the windows. She was still too leery to simply step outside, but she peered through the glass. Three sides of the house seemed to be surrounded by trees. The front opened up to a view of a long glen. No other houses or other signs of human habitation were visible beyond the long driveway that led down to the road. Instead of making her feel isolated and anxious, the lack of neighbors made her feel safe. Or maybe that was Ewan himself. In less than a day, he'd managed to make her feel protected for the first time since her mother died, and that was no small thing.

As if summoned by her thoughts, his Land Rover turned in at the end of the drive.

She looked down at herself in the borrowed shirt, stomach twisting into knots of worry. But before she could rush to the guest room to change, the front door was opening, and Ewan strode inside with a duffel bag. He spotted her by the window.

His gaze slid over her, lingering for a moment on the shirt. "Christ, you're a wee thing. Hopefully, something in here will fit you better."

Knots loosening, she took the bag he offered. "Where did this come from?"

Something that might have been sheepishness flickered over his face. "I borrowed them from my sister."

Isobel tensed. "Someone else knows I'm here?"

"I didnae give details. No' even your name. But Ciara knows when and how to be discreet, and she'll do whatever she can to help. Including hiding the fact that I've got anyone here."

With no other choice, she had to trust his judgment. If he believed his sister was safe, she probably was. On a slow exhale, Isobel loosed the death grip she'd taken on the bag. "That probably won't last very long, will it?"

"No. I'm expected back from my trip on Monday. Someone will come looking for me within a day or so. But you'll get the opportunity to recover more from your injuries, and we can see about finding you a place and getting you settled in before coming into work."

She found herself disappointed that her place wouldn't be here with him. But she said nothing. The man had gone so far out of his way for her, and that was far more than she had any right to expect. Still, that wasn't the only issue.

"Certainly, I appreciate the job, but there's the small matter that I haven't had time to earn a paycheck. And I don't know if I can afford rent anywhere. I don't have access to any of my accounts." Heat bloomed in her cheeks. For all that Paul had controlled the purse strings, she hadn't ever had to worry about money. Not that she was afraid to live in impoverished circumstances, but she truly didn't know how she'd be able to afford the basics.

"Dinna worry about that. Glenlaig isnae the sort of place where you have to worry about a deposit and last month's rent on top of the regular rent. And I'm certain I can arrange something week-to-week if needed." He stopped himself, rocking back on his heels as if he realized he'd been railroading her. "If that's still what you want."

As he spoke, she'd opened the bag and sifted through the contents, noting not only the expected basics, but real pajamas, socks, comfortable shoes, toiletries, and even an unopened toothbrush. For some reason, the sight of that toothbrush had a knot of tears clogging her throat. By some miracle, she'd landed somewhere with good people. She'd be a fool to turn away their help.

Swallowing down her emotions, she strove for calm. "Yes, I'd like to take you up on all of it."

His head jerked in a brusque nod. "Okay. I'll work on finding you a place. And I promise you I willnae let you go anywhere that isn't safe."

Isobel wasn't sure anywhere could be truly safe, but she understood he believed it, so she'd try. "Thank you."

"There's just one more thing."

She braced herself. "And that is?"

"We need to decide on your cover story. Who you are. Why you're here. Where you came from. You're new, so people will ask, and it'll be better if you have an answer, so you dinna fumble."

"That makes sense. I'll put the kettle on." She stopped herself after half a step. "If that's all right?"

That craggy face softened a fraction. "You dinna have to ask. It's fine. Tea's in the cannister on the counter. Make yourself at home."

Isobel had no idea how to do that, but at least she could make tea.

SOME CONVERSATIONS WERE BETTER HAD in person.

That was part of what had prompted Ewan to drive out to see his cousin, Connor MacKean, at the family estate of Ardinmuir. Estate made it sound like they were rolling in money, when, in fact, Connor and his sister had been struggling for years to make the ancestral castle and surrounding lands profitable. Only since Kyla's marriage last year, to Texan Raleigh Beaumont, had the tide begun to turn. Raleigh, the new baron of the neighboring estate of Lochmara, had come up with the rather brilliant suggestion of converting the empty crofter's cottages on both estates into vacation rentals. Ewan was hoping they'd have an empty one.

It wasn't his first choice. His instinct was to keep Isobel with him, especially after what Conroy had turned up. He knew he could keep her safe. But she hadn't asked for a bodyguard, and they'd already be working together at the pub. She deserved to have her own space, to make her own choices. He didn't want to hold her captive in any way that reminded her of the life she'd escaped. Not even in the name of safety. More than that, he didn't want her to feel any more beholden to him for the help he'd given her.

Over the past couple of days, signs of the concussion had faded. She still had some headaches and tenderness, but she was healing well and seemed more comfortable on that front. Even the bruising on her wrist was improving. But she was still skittish and had said nothing personal about herself. If she truly stuck around, that would simply take time. She'd worried about making tea, for Chrissakes. Her head had been fucked with well beyond any physical abuse.

But she didn't seem to be afraid of him. He'd take that as progress.

Out of long habit, he pulled his 4x4 around to the back side of the castle, parking near the kitchen door, though the lack of other vehicles suggested they weren't running some sort of event this weekend. Ardinmuir Event Planning had been the brainchild of Kyla and her best friend Sophie. Ewan didn't know how Connor stood having his home invaded by strangers on the regular, for the weddings and other parties hosted here. Then again, he was so in love with Sophie, he'd likely do anything with a smile.

With a perfunctory knock, Ewan strode into the kitchen. It felt oddly empty without Connor's great uncle Angus at the counter mixing up some sort of confection. He was down in Berkshire as a competitor on the latest season of *The Great British Bake Off,* and they were all cheering him on from here, dying to know how far he'd make it. Finding no sign of his cousin, he wandered through the castle, checking all the usual haunts. He was starting to think he'd have to drive out to Connor's forge to track him down, when he overheard voices coming from the library.

With another quick knock, he let himself in to find Connor, his very pregnant sister Kyla, Raleigh, Sophie, and Raleigh's adoptive mother, Charlotte, who managed all the rental cottages across both estates.

"Ewan! You're back!" Connor's smile flashed so bright, Ewan nearly recoiled.

"Aye. Did you miss me that much?"

His cousin laughed. "It has been damned quiet around here with Angus gone. Family dinners havenae been the same without everyone."

"Oh, but that's not why he's so happy," Charlotte drawled.

Ewan just arched a brow and waited for someone to clue him in.

Sophie rose from her seat and moved to slip an arm around Connor, lifting her left hand to display the flash of a ring there.

Ewan just blinked at it. She'd been wearing that ring for months as part of the fake engagement she'd entered into at the start of the year because of a complicated situation arising from Connor's former playboy past and a threat to the event planning business. In the end, it hadn't been much of a threat, but a real relationship had grown out of the deception.

"We're engaged," she explained.

"Oh? For real this time?"

Sophie beamed. "Absolutely for real this time."

"My beautiful, wonderful Sophie said yes, and I plan to lock her down before she changes her mind." Connor stole a smacking kiss that had her laughter rolling out.

"We're combining a bit of work with pleasure and celebrating." Kyla lifted a glass of something orange and sparkly. "Well, they are. I'm stuck with fizzy juice."

Raleigh rubbed her shoulders. "Just a few more weeks, darlin'."

"Can't be soon enough. I'm going completely stir crazy. Sophie and Ciara have officially put me on maternity leave, whether I like it or not. I know I can't walk much, but my brain still works. Mostly." She rubbed at the mound of her baby belly.

"I'm just ready for this baby to *get here already*. I'm tired of being fat and swollen and miserable."

Miserable himself at this turn of the conversation, Ewan could only manage, "Uh…"

Connor snickered and clapped him on the shoulder. "Pour you a drink, cousin?"

"No. Thanks. I had something I wanted to talk to you about. All of you, I guess." He understood Isobel's reservations about bringing more people into the circle, but these were *his* people, and he trusted them implicitly. They were family. "I need your help."

The room fell silent, and more than one jaw dropped. Ewan shifted in discomfort. He was the guy who gave help. He never asked for it. But this wasn't something he could manage entirely on his own. With a deep breath, he launched in. After much discussion, he and Isobel had elected to stick as close to the truth as possible. He'd rescued her from a car accident during the storm. She was escaping from an abusive relationship. He knew the natural assumption would be that the relationship was romantic, and they'd decided it would be easiest to allow people to run with that.

"Bless her heart. I'd like to get my hands on that son of a bitch." Charlotte's ready defense didn't surprise him at all. She had a tendency to mother everybody and was notorious for collecting strays. He had a feeling Isobel could do with some of her brand of mothering.

"You and me both," Ewan agreed. "Anyway, she's staying here for a while. I'm hiring her on at the pub, and she'll need somewhere to stay. I dinna ken how long, so I was hoping there might be an option somewhere on the estate that could be let on a week-to-week basis."

"I'm sure we've got something that will suit." Kyla looked at Charlotte, who frowned.

"Off the top of my head, I don't have anything immediately

available. Most of the cottages between both estates are booked through the entire summer. At least, for all the weekends. But we might have some other options over at Lochmara."

"There are certainly tons of rooms here in the castle. She's welcome to stay with us," Sophie offered.

There was some appeal to that, in the sense that people he trusted would be here. But Ewan didn't want to just dump Isobel off in a place with strangers.

"Let me get back home, where I have access to the full reservation system, and see what I can come up with," Charlotte said. "We'll meet tomorrow and take a tour of the options."

"That would be much appreciated. What time? I'm due at the pub mid-afternoon."

"Say around ten in the morning? That'll give us time to drive around, as needed."

"Good. And let's just do it you and us, aye? I dinna want to overwhelm her with too many new people at once. She's skittish. Justifiably so."

When they all stared at him, he went brows up. "What?"

Connor shrugged. "Nothing. It's just you havenae been involved with anyone since you came home."

"Isobel and I are no' involved. She just needs help. Someone to keep her safe. I can do that." Ewan had the general sense that no one had taken on that role since her mother died. He wondered what had happened to her father, but hadn't asked yet. She was only just starting to get more relaxed and comfortable, and he didn't want to rock the boat or push for too much, too fast.

When they only kept staring, he folded his arms. "It's the right thing to do."

"Nobody's doubting your honor, baby," Charlotte soothed. "That big heart is absolutely in the right place."

She didn't bat an eye at the stare he leveled on her. Tough woman was Charlotte.

"Right, well, that'll be settled soon enough. We're all happy to help however we can." Connor moved to the sideboard and pulled out another lowball. "In the meantime, I insist you join us for a celebratory toast."

Understanding the need for this ritual, Ewan figured he could take the time for one drink before he headed home. Isobel was fine at his place for a while longer.

"Fine. But I'm pouring."

## 5

I sobel paced the house, trying to work off the prickle of anxiety. Ewan had said he'd be back in a few hours. He had to check on some things at the pub before meeting with someone about rental property. There was no reason to believe anyone knew where she was. She was safe here. She believed that. Mostly. But that was harder to hang onto when he wasn't nearby, exuding confidence and competence like some kind of protective force field.

*Best get used to it, girl. He's not going to be nearby when you move into your new place. Wherever that ends up being.*

Knowing she'd keep spinning if she didn't find something to do, she wandered into the kitchen and began poking around in the fridge and cabinets. Maybe she could make him dinner as a thank you for everything he'd done. Given the life she'd led, her kitchen skills weren't exactly gourmet. But there were still a few things she made from time to time, when she had the option, because it reminded her of cooking with her mother when she was young. She could handle some stew and a round of soda bread.

Pleased with the idea, she began hunting up ingredients,

piling onions, potatoes, and carrots on the counter. She found a pound of minced lamb in the freezer and a box of chicken stock in a cabinet. The rhythm of scrubbing, peeling, and chopping soothed her nerves. There was pleasure in making a simple meal for someone who mattered. No, she hadn't known Ewan long and didn't know him well, but he gave a damn about her, so that made him important.

The stew had come to a simmer, and she'd just slipped the round of bread dough into the oven, when the front door opened.

Isobel turned, expecting to see Ewan, and instead spotted an enormous white dog. The dog zeroed in on her and woofed, bounding toward her. On a gasp, she backpedaled, but found her retreat blocked by the counter. The animal's tail wagged like an out-of-control metronome, its tongue hanging out in an expression that looked for all the world like a smile as he skidded to a stop in front of her. He was so big, his head came almost to her sternum. But he didn't seem like he wanted to eat her. Isobel offered a tentative hand. The dog sniffed and immediately nudged her palm with his big head, demanding pets. She obliged with a scratch between his floppy ears, loosening enough to laugh when he groaned in pleasure and leaned into her. If not for the counter at her back, she'd have fallen right over from the bulk of him.

"Making friends already, Havoc? Dinna knock the poor woman over, you dolt."

Isobel's head snapped toward the unfamiliar voice to find a woman standing in the entryway. Her breath backed up in her throat, and her fingers instinctively curled in the dog's slightly coarse fur.

Seemingly oblivious to her panic, the other woman stepped further into the room, dropping some bags on the floor. "You must be my brother's guest. I'm Ciara. And that great big love there is Havoc."

"Oh." It was all she could manage as she fought not to sink to the floor with relief in the wake of the adrenaline dump. She could see the resemblance now, in the shape of Ciara's eyes and the wave of her dark brown hair. And it made sense. She was the only other person who knew Isobel was here.

Ciara studied her, finally seeming to register her discomfort. "I came over to bring this lad back. I didnae realize Ewan wouldn't be here. I probably startled you, just walking on in like that. I'm sorry."

"It's... fine." Havoc pressed closer to her legs, seeming to sense her distress. She dug both hands into the thick fur of his ruff and felt more grounded. "He'll be back in a little while."

"Just as well. I brought something for you."

"For me? You've already done so much with the loan of clothes and toiletries and... everything. I really appreciate all of it. That was very kind of you."

"Of course." Ciara curled a hand around the back of one of the kitchen chairs. "Look, my brother told me a little bit about what you're going through. I know you need to lie low—and feel free to reject this as an option—but part of lying low effectively would be not looking the same as you did when you left... wherever you left."

"What do you mean?"

"Well, that hair of yours is beautiful, but also pretty distinctive. The first option is to dye it." She opened one of the shopping bags and pulled out several boxes. "These are all semipermanent, so they'll wash out over time. But it would make you look a whole lot different. If you're going to be working in the pub with the public, that seems like it could be important."

Isobel could see the sense in that. No one knew her here, but her music was internationally renowned. Her everyday look was different from the professionally done makeup and hair, but it was still possible someone could recognize her from an album cover. She'd never dyed her hair before. Paul wouldn't have allowed it, so there was an additional appeal to being able to make the choice to do something different. "It's a good thought."

"I wasn't sure what you'd prefer or what would go with your skin tone, so I brought a variety." Ciara dumped a myriad of boxes out on the kitchen table.

Relaxing, Isobel moved to join her, and together they reviewed the options for what might work best and look the most natural.

"Hmm. With your complexion, you could go red or brown. The brown would be more subtle."

"Subtle is good."

"I dinna have enough of any one color, given your hair is so long." She reached forward, plucking up a few boxes. "But we can mix these two different browns and have enough. The color will come out somewhere between."

Isobel eyed the boxes warily. "Are you sure it's safe to do that?"

"Oh, aye. My girlfriends and I used to play with hair colors all the time in uni. These are both dyes, not bleaches. Same brand and same level of permanence. Plus, mixing the two gives you a more believable color." She nodded. "Let's do this."

"What? Now?"

"No time like the present. Here. I brought some old clothes that won't get damaged if we drip a wee bit."

Feeling a little steamrolled, Isobel offered the only protest she could think of. "But I've got bread in the oven."

"There's a timer set, aye? If you're in the shower when it needs to come out, I can pull it." Ciara was already grabbing glass bowls from the cabinet to mix things.

On a deep breath, Isobel gave herself over to the experience and went to change clothes. Ewan's sister was a cheerful, chatty woman. As she applied the color, she kept up a running commentary about her friends from university and the two jobs she was working now that she was out—a server at her broth-er's pub and a part-time event planner at the company owned by their cousin, Kyla. Isobel didn't even try to keep up with the cast of characters she mentioned. It was far too overwhelming. But the talking helped pass the time and kept Isobel from giving in to her anxiety. Plus, the whole thing was kind of... fun. She'd never had girlfriends before. She imagined it might be something like this. If she stayed in Glenlaig, maybe there could be more of this kind of interaction.

When the time was up, Ciara sent her to wash out the dye, along with a warning not to look in the mirror after. "If we're gonna do this thing, you need to at least get to enjoy the surprise reveal."

Because it added to the sense of fun, Isobel did as she asked, coming out a little while later, redressed in normal clothes and combing out her wet hair.

Ciara took one look at her and nodded, satisfied. "Aye, that's going to be very different. It'll make your eyes pop. That's a great start. There is one other thing we can do."

"What's that?"

"Do you trust me?" She held up a pair of scissors.

"You want to cut my hair? I'm not sure about that."

"I'm not talking about anything drastic. But that length is still very noticeable. If we take some of it off... say, just past your shoulders, it would be a dramatic change and give you some options for hairstyles you probably can't pull off right now. I've done basic cuts on my girlfriends, too. Just simple, more or less straight cuts. Lightly layered. Maybe with some curtain bangs."

As the coloring had, it made sense. Isobel had kept the same hairstyle for years. And, well, if it wasn't great, it would grow. It was just hair.

"Okay."

Ciara grinned, and Isobel found herself smiling back.

"Have a seat in my chair."

The first snip of scissors had her gut clenching. The sight of that long curl of brown on the floor actually made her whimper.

"Maybe you should close your eyes."

"Good idea."

So she did, trying to listen to Ciara's stories instead of the sound of more and more of her hair being cut from her head. Her fingers gripped the edge of the chair.

"Okay, now I'm just going to finish it out with the dryer. I brought one along because I'm positive my brother doesn't own such an appliance."

Isobel had spent hours of her life in a chair, having her hair and makeup done by professionals. But none of that felt as... good as this. If she didn't think too hard about the why of all of it, the experience almost felt like a sort of pampering. Almost. Because it came with the side of what felt like shades of friendship.

At last, the dryer cut off. "Okay. Now for the reveal."

Ciara thrust a hand mirror in front of Isobel's face. Pulling back a little, she took it and focused on the reflection.

"Wow."

Ciara had been right. She looked dramatically different like this. The darker hair color played well against her fair skin and made her changeable eyes look more green. Certainly, anyone who actually knew her and was looking for such a change would be able to tell it was her, but for someone who was just casually glancing? Chances were, they wouldn't immediately recognize her. The cut framed her face, highlighting the shape of it in a way that made her look older, even without the aid of makeup. As a bonus, the swoop of bangs covered the still healing cut on her brow. The whole thing was wonderful.

"What did you do?"

At the snap of Ewan's voice, she nearly bobbled the mirror. Neither of them had heard him come inside.

Ciara took the mirror. "We gave her a makeover. Now she's much less recognizable. If she's going to be working with the public at the pub, that's going to be important."

With a growing sense of dread, Isobel turned toward him. He stood in the entryway, staring at her, the dog head-butting his belly for attention.

"Aye. You do look different."

She couldn't read his tone, and that worried her.

"I brought Havoc and all his stuff back. I assume things went well with Connor?"

"Connor?" The question slipped out before Isobel could stop it.

"Our other cousin. Kyla's brother," Ciara explained.

"Aye. Tomorrow we're going to look at some options for flats between Ardinmuir and Lochmara."

"Oh, that'll be a great place for her. It's beautiful out there. And now I'm going to get out of your way. Isobel, it was lovely to meet you. I look forward to seeing you at the pub."

With as much whirlwind efficiency as she'd arrived, Ciara packed up her things and left.

Havoc abandoned his master and came back to press against Isobel when she rose from the chair. Again, she threaded her fingers into his ruff.

Ewan was still staring at her, and she fought not to curl in on herself when she couldn't read him.

"I'm sorry."

His brows drew together. "For what?"

She had no idea. Apologizing was simply what she habitually did when she wasn't certain about how someone was feeling or behaving. "I... You seem upset."

He shook himself, that thundercloud expression softening. "No. No, it was a good idea, and it's your right to make whatever decision you want. I just wasnae expecting her to be here. You definitely dinna look like the same person."

His gaze slid over her again, up and down, before he jerked it away. "Do I smell food?"

*Was he checking me out? Surely not.*

Dismissing the thought as ridiculous, she moved toward the kitchen. "I made lamb stew and some soda bread. I don't have a lot of cooking skills, but I can manage some simple things."

That stoic facade cracked into a look of wonder. "You cooked for me?"

Isobel suppressed the urge to apologize again. "It seemed like a nice gesture. As a thank you for... everything."

His stomach let out a massive growl. "That smells fair brilliant. When do we eat?"

Feeling more on even ground, she grabbed some bowls. "Right now."

From the driver's seat, Ewan glanced over at Isobel, noting the way her fingers curled white round the edge of her seat. "Nervous?"

Her gaze darted to him. "A little."

"Charlotte can be... a lot. But she's one of the kindest people I know. She's the one who'll be showing us around this morning."

"How much does she know?"

"Only what you and I agreed to. It's enough. You can count on her discretion, and everyone else's. They're all good people."

She nodded and turned her gaze out the window.

As a rule, Ewan had no issue with silence. In most cases, he preferred it. But he was hyperaware of everything about Isobel this morning, knowing this was a big step for her and wanting to make it as easy as it could be. That wasn't the only reason for his focus.

That whole makeover his sister had orchestrated might

have made her less recognizable, but it also made it impossible not to notice Isobel as a woman. A very attractive woman. Okay, he'd noticed that before the makeover. But she'd seemed so young to begin with. And she was. At twenty-four, she was only a couple years older than Ciara. But with clothes that fit and the new hair, it was harder to remember that.

Putting some space between them would be a good idea. Isobel was vulnerable and, in a sense, dependent on him. He wasn't about to put strings on that or do anything at all to inadvertently prey upon her. Getting her into her own space, where she wouldn't be across the hall when he woke from dreams that left him hard and aching with a desire that absolutely wasn't going to be satisfied, had to be a priority.

As they crested a hill, Ardinmuir came into view. "Holy crap! Is that a castle?" The delight in her voice made him relax.

"Aye. That's my cousins' place."

Her head whipped toward him. "Seriously?"

"Aye. Connor and Kyla are my cousins on their mother's side. Ardinmuir came down on their father's side. There've been MacKeans inhabiting it for centuries."

"They grew up in *a castle?*"

"We all did, in a sense. Ciara less so, as she's a fair bit younger. But Connor, Kyla, and I are closer in age. I spent a lot of my boyhood tromping these woods and exploring the castle. We made up all sorts of adventures." And, damn, he hadn't thought about any of that in years.

"What a lovely memory to have of childhood."

The wistful note in her voice had him glancing over again. "No castles and forests in yours?"

"I didn't have much of a childhood."

The statement was matter-of-fact, and it sparked a dozen questions of why. Conroy had gathered more data on her in his search, but Ewan hadn't let him reveal anything that wasn't directly pertinent to her immediate safety. He felt bad enough about maintaining the subterfuge that he had no idea who she was. He'd let her reveal herself to him at her own pace.

"Are we going up there?"

"Not today, no. But certainly another time, if you like. Connor can give you a tour. Kyla's better, but she canna do the walk just now."

"Is she injured?"

It worried him that her brain immediately went to someone being hurt. "No, just verra, verra pregnant."

"Oh."

They lapsed back into silence as he wound his way into the woods to the first stop on the list Charlotte had texted him.

She was waiting in front of the little cottage, her wide and welcoming smile flashing white against her tan skin as they climbed out. "Good mornin'. You must be Isobel. I'm Charlotte Vasquez."

Isobel blinked and accepted her hand for a shake. "You're… Southern? Is that Texas I'm hearing?"

Ewan stared at her. How the hell could she pick out a Texas accent?

"It is, and I am. You've spent some time in the States?"

Isobel hummed an affirmative and offered nothing more. "And how does a woman from Texas end up living here?"

"Oh, well, that's a story. The short version is that my adopted son won a barony in a poker game and ended up marrying Ewan's cousin Kyla to keep it—on account of the three-hundred-year-old marriage pact that said they'd both lose their estates if they didn't. I followed him over."

Isobel's mouth opened, then closed again as she shot a glance at him for confirmation.

He nodded. "Aye, that's the gist of it. It was complicated."

"I feel like someone needs to tell me the longer version, at some point."

Charlotte laughed. "I'm sure that can be arranged. Come on inside, and I'll give y'all the tour."

Ewan brought up the rear, eyes automatically scanning the layout of the little one-bedroom cottage. He'd helped with renovations on quite a few of them, but not this particular unit. There were two doors, one in the front that they'd just entered through, and one in the back, leading out to the woods. As Charlotte prattled on about the features of the place—the wee kitchen, the cozy bath, the privacy—he evaluated the security. And found it lacking. Nestled in the trees as it was, there were too many easy approaches. And the very lack of nearby cottages meant somebody could sneak up and snatch Isobel from either side, and no one would be any the wiser.

"No."

At his clipped statement, Charlotte cut off her spiel. "No?"

"Too isolated. It'd be too easy to sneak up and snatch her. Next."

Ewan regretted his brusque tone as Isobel lost a few shades of color from her cheeks.

"Well, that's all right. We've got a couple more."

They loaded into their respective vehicles and caravanned to the next cottage on the list. This one was part of Lochmara's holdings. Instead of the quiet forest, this cottage was perched along the crest of a hill in a row of three others that overlooked the rolling green pastures dotted with sheep. Even as they slid out of the Land Rover, Ewan was shaking his head.

"You haven't even seen it yet," Charlotte protested.

"It's too close to the other rentals. There'd be guests coming and going regularly from the other cottages with a clear view of this one. Unless you'll consent to running a background screening on the other guests to ensure they're not a problem?"

"Guests?" Isobel asked.

"They're vacation rentals. That's one of the primary sources of income for both Lochmara and Ardinmuir. But okay. I see Ewan's point. Load up. We've got one more."

Isobel said nothing as they drove closer to the manor house at Lochmara, but Ewan felt compelled to fill the silence with a defense of his proclamations.

"I promised I wouldnae see you settled anywhere I didnae think you'd be safe. It's entirely possible I'm being over-protective. I'm a paranoid bastard. But I canna stand the idea of seeing you hurt again." *And I dinna fully ken what I'm protecting you from.* He kept that last thought to himself.

Surprise flickered over her features as she glanced his way. "I appreciate your concern. Truly."

Following Charlotte, they drove on past the manor house.

"I feel like the Bennet sisters should be walking out that front door."

"Who?"

"From *Pride and Prejudice.* Never mind. Are those people playing fetch with... a cow?"

Ewan looked over to the nearby pasture, where Raleigh was winging a huge ball. A shaggy brown form lumbered after it, while a smaller black-and-white dog ran zoomies around the perimeter. From her perch in a chair on the outside of the fence, Kyla threw back her head and laughed.

"Aye. That's Mabel. She's a Highland Coo that Raleigh and Kyla rescued as a wee calf. She lived in the house for a while. Thinks she's a dog. Her wee companion there is Dugal."

Ewan frowned as Charlotte parked near the barn. Her other adopted son, Gavin, poked his head out, along with her partner, Malcolm, the estate manager for Lochmara. This wasn't what they'd agreed to. It was too many people, too soon. But he parked and got out, circling around to flank Isobel.

As everyone's heads swiveled in their direction, she took a step closer to him, and he couldn't stop himself from settling a hand on the small of her back. She eased at the touch.

*Dinna read anything into it. You're just the most familiar person here.*

"It'll be fine," he murmured.

She moved forward with him, slipping on a calm mask that would've fooled even him, had he not spent the past few days with her.

"I'll make introductions," Charlotte announced. "This is my fiancé, Malcolm Niall, and our boy, Gavin. And my eldest boy, Raleigh Beaumont, and his wife, Kyla MacKean. Everybody, this is Isobel. I'm sorry. I don't know your last name."

"Donnchadh."

Malcolm rocked back on his heels. "I knew a Donnchadh once. From up near Aberdeen. Do you have kin up that way?"

The easy question seemed to both surprise and amuse Isobel. "Not that I'm aware." She didn't offer the expected details about where she was from, but nobody pressed.

"Ewan has security concerns about the cottages for this particular situation."

Feeling a little defensive, he folded his arms.

Unruffled, Charlotte strolled toward the back side of the manor house, to the row of buildings that extended along the perimeter of the formal gardens. "Our last option is the duplex. Malcolm and I actually lived on either side of it before we moved out to our house with Gavin earlier this spring. It's close to the main house but still has privacy. We don't house guests on this part of the estate, and there will be plenty of us around to keep an eye out for you."

She no doubt intended for that to be a comforting statement, but Ewan caught the hitch in Isobel's step.

"No." The word slipped out before he could think better of it.

Isobel swung around to look at him, brows up. "No?"

He just shook his head. Everyone was staring. He didn't look at them, but he could feel their eyes on him.

Isobel flashed a faint, placating smile toward Charlotte. "Can you excuse us for just a moment?"

"Of course."

When her arm slid through his, towing him out of earshot from the group, Ewan didn't resist. He was too busy cataloging the feel of her touch on his arm.

"What's the problem with this one?"

How could he explain that the biggest problem was that it wasn't near him? He flexed his fists, wrestling with his instincts and his conscience.

"Correct me if I'm wrong, but aren't we running out of options?"

"There's one more that makes more sense than any of these."

"Okay, then let's do that. You said you'd find the best option."

"It's staying with me." He ground the words out.

"Oh." She swallowed and seemed to fold in on herself. "I'm sorry. I don't want to put you out. I've inconvenienced you enough."

Hating that the brief glimpse of ease and confidence had disappeared, he started to reach for her and stopped himself. "No. It's no' putting me out. I'm no' upset at the idea of you staying with me. I just dinna want to pressure you. You've had enough of that." He sucked in a slow breath. "In the end, it's your decision. I willnae tell you what to do or force you into anything."

She blinked up at him, those gorgeous eyes searching his. "You wouldn't mind having me stay?"

"No. It would be simplest. I ken I can protect you if you're with me. But you dinna have to. You deserve to have your own space."

"I'd like to stay. If it's truly all right with you. I do feel safer with you."

All the tension that had lodged in his gut evaporated. "Then it's official. We'll be housemates."

Isobel nodded, her lips curving into a shy little smile that made him feel like he'd won the bloody lottery.

He was in so much trouble. But he nodded anyway, because this was what he'd wanted. "All right. We'll go tell the others."

They strode back to where his friends and family were making zero effort not to watch.

He opened his mouth to speak, but Charlotte beat him to it.

"She's going to stay with you."

Too surprised by the announcement, he just nodded.

She grinned like a cat who'd gotten into the cream. "I had a feeling. Welcome to Glenlaig, Isobel."

## 6

"I have to go into the pub for the night."

Isobel accepted Ewan's announcement with equanimity. "I did assume you'd eventually have to get back to your actual life."

"You're welcome to come. You'll want to meet everybody before you actually start there yourself, but I thought you might have had enough excitement for the day."

"You're not wrong. I'll be fine. Havoc will keep me company."

Hearing his name, the big dog rubbed his head against her hip.

"I'm thinkin' you've acquired a friend for life. I've never seen him take to someone like this."

"I have a confession to make."

Ewan's expression carefully blanked, and she felt bad for making him think she was about to confide in him about anything big.

"I'm kind of in love with your dog."

If he was disappointed she'd chosen to keep things light and surface, he didn't show it. One corner of his mouth kicked up in amusement. "I'd say the feeling is mutual. As he's got a champion beggar face, I'll tell you he's no' to have anything processed or we'll end up with a mess to clean up. There was an incident with tinned chili we willnae speak of. But he's verra fond of cheese."

Isobel felt her own lips twitch. "Noted."

"It's a weeknight, so the pub closes at ten. If I can shake loose earlier than that, I will. It'll just depend on how busy we are."

"It's fine. I'll be okay."

He fidgeted for another moment, which seemed so at odds with his usual self-possession she almost asked if *he'd* be okay.

Finally, he nodded to himself. "Right. I'm off. And remember that this is your place now, too. Make yourself comfortable."

"Thanks."

Then he was gone, the door clicking shut behind him.

Isobel looked down at Havoc. "Well, it's just you and me tonight. What shall we do with ourselves?"

He trailed her through the house as she explored more thoroughly. Ewan had wanted her to stay. Had outright shot down all the other alternatives. Isobel didn't read too much into that. Maybe they really were rife with security risks. Or maybe it was simply easier for him to keep an eye on her and the situation if she stayed close. Still, the idea that this could be her place, too, at least for a while, gave her comfort. It made her feel as if she really could do this. Start over here. With Ewan.

Well, not *with* Ewan. He didn't look at her like that. But with him as an ally.

After seeing a couple of the cottages today, she realized that his house must have been of the same vintage. She could see a similar floor plan here, only a little larger, as if it had been added onto at some point. There were three bedrooms—his, the guest room where she'd been sleeping, and a third room he'd turned into a home gym. A second, smaller bathroom with only a shower and pedestal sink was tucked in there. The kitchen opened to the lounge area, and this was where the addition had pushed out. It was an economical use of space. Or maybe that was just the sparse furniture. As he'd said, it was only him.

That was fine. No matter what she was used to, she hadn't come from affluence in the beginning.

Briefly, she considered turning on the TV or radio for some noise. But she was too afraid of what news reports might be saying about the disappearance of Elizabeth Duncan before a sold-out concert. Perhaps this ostrich routine was foolish. She ought to know what was being said. What was being done. But without a phone or computer, she had no other way of looking into it. There was no asking Ewan or Ciara without revealing who she truly was. For a little while longer, she just wanted to stay safe in her bubble.

Without someone else to cook for, she elected to make a charcuterie spread for dinner, cutting up cheese and meats, adding some raw vegetables with a dip she found in the fridge. Then she settled onto the couch with a book she'd pulled from the shelves, Havoc curled up beside her, staring with big, hopeful eyes.

"Do you want to tell me how it is your da has romance novels in his collection? Because he doesn't seem like the sort of person who'd read romance."

Havoc's tail thumped, and his gaze slid to the plate of food on the end table.

"That's your price, hmm?" Conscious of Ewan's warning, she plucked one of the pieces of cheese she'd cut into extra tiny bites and offered it. Havoc neatly nipped it from her fingers. She'd never had a pet before. With her lifestyle, it hadn't made sense. But it was lovely to share food and cuddles with the big dog.

They'd wiped out the simple meal—Havoc getting a fair amount of the cheese—and Isobel had made it several chapters into a fish-out-of-water small town romance about a city guy who'd inherited a failing bookstore from his grandmother, when someone knocked on the door.

The book tumbled from her hands and anxiety shot through her system.

*It's fine. There's no possible way Paul could know where I am.*

Swallowing, she uncurled from the couch and moved toward the door. Havoc's bulk beside her was a comfort. She had no idea if he'd get aggressive with a threat, but just his sheer size would make someone think twice. Curling her hand in his fur, she checked through the peephole. Ciara stood on the other side of the door.

The panic ebbed. She opened the door and found not just Ewan's sister, but also Charlotte, Kyla, and a gorgeous Indian woman with the most striking grey eyes she'd ever seen. The four of them were loaded down with bags and boxes.

"What is all this?"

Ciara nudged past her, leading the way with a stack of cartons. "I know exactly how spare my brother lives. No woman wants to suffer in that kind of environment. You're staying here, so you deserve to be comfortable, and we're here to see to that."

"I don't understand."

Across the room, Charlotte was pulling what looked like throw pillows out of a bag. "Just consider us the welcome wagon, sugar."

The fourth woman offered a gentle smile. "I'm Sophie. Connor's fiancée. I'm here to provide the plants." To illustrate the point, she offloaded a couple of... well, Isobel had no idea what they were. She knew about as much about gardening as she did how to waitress.

As they all trooped back outside, Kyla lowered herself into

one of the kitchen chairs. "I'm here for moral support and to provide dessert. It's the only thing they'll let me do."

Overwhelmed, Isobel could only watch as they worked together in a seamless unit, putting out pillows and throw blankets, placing plants, and setting out decorative bowls and vases. Ciara and Charlotte even brought in furniture, adding a bedside table to her room, and a small chest of drawers. When they began hanging things on the empty wall, she wondered if she ought to protest, but she had a feeling they wouldn't listen.

Forty-five minutes later, Charlotte balled her hands on generous hips. "There. That's much better."

Isobel looked around at all the softening touches they'd added that warmed the space immeasurably. "You just... had all of this lying around?"

Ciara folded her arms. "I have been waiting for *two years* to get my hands on my brother's place. You are the perfect excuse to make this a home."

Isobel had no idea how she felt about that. And she definitely didn't know how *Ewan* would feel about this invasion and the addition of all this stuff to the house. It was his space. He had every right to be minimalist, if that was his preference. Still, she was touched that these women had wanted so badly for her to feel at home and welcome here. It felt like the first tendrils of friendship.

Swallowing against the tightness in her throat, she looked at each of them. "You don't even know me."

"That's okay," Kyla assured her. "We don't have to. Your story is yours to tell whenever you're ready. Just know that we're looking forward to getting to know you."

"For sure," Ciara concurred. "Anybody who can blast my brother out of the rut he's been living in is someone I want to know."

Isobel wasn't sure how to take that. Was she implying he was interested in her romantically? Isobel started to protest, then decided against it. If that wasn't what Ciara had meant, she'd look foolish.

"Now that the work is done, I say we break out the cake," Sophie suggested.

"There's cake?" Isobel had a serious soft spot for cake and had rarely been able to indulge.

"In this family, there's almost always something sweet," Kyla explained. "Someone bring me a knife."

They divvied up the lemon drizzle cake and sat around the living room, talking and laughing. Conversation flowed around Isobel, without much need for her to contribute. She had nothing to add to the discussion of Charlotte and Malcolm's upcoming wedding or when Sophie and her man Connor should try to set the date, but she didn't feel excluded. They were open to her contributions when she made them, and otherwise didn't pressure her. It was really lovely to be in the company of women. She'd had occasional tastes of this among some of the musicians she traveled with. But Paul had usually put a stop to it, undermining her efforts to be friendly and make connections.

*Paul's not here. And there's nothing stopping you from being friends with these women, if you want.*

And she did.

When the door opened again, Isobel only noticed because Havoc popped up.

Ewan came inside, his dark brows knit. "What...?"

Ciara headed off whatever argument he might've made. "We brought all of this over for Isobel, so whatever protests you have, you just shove them on down. You are no longer the only person to live here, brother. She deserves some comforts, and I dinna care whether you need them or not. You're going to live with it."

At the defiant lift of her chin, he shut his mouth and looked at Isobel.

She recognized his silent question about whether she was okay and nodded.

For several long, silent moments, his gaze scanned the space, taking in all the new additions before landing on the plates with a few bites remaining. "Fine. Is there more cake?"

Ciara flashed a triumphant grin. "There is. And since you're not making a big stink about this, you can have some."

By Wednesday afternoon, Ewan was satisfied that the worst of Isobel's concussion symptoms were healed. Only the faintest hint of bruising remained at her temple and along her wrist, and she insisted she had full function and range of motion. So it was time to bring her more fully into his world and introduce her to his pub family. Which also meant introducing her to Glenlaig. Other than his house, she'd only seen Ardinmuir from a distance and a little of Lochmara. If she was to make a real life here, she needed to start getting to know the village itself.

As they passed the old stone church on the way into town, Isobel gasped and pressed closer to the window, trying to look everywhere at once. "Oh, this is adorable."

Ewan focused on the village himself, noting the familiar buildings and the faint gleam of wet on the cobbled high street from the morning's rain. All the things he'd taken little notice of because it was simply home. What did she see? Was this redolent of home for her, or was it like the set of a stage play? Some novelty that she'd grow weary of in time?

Conscious of not pressuring her for answers she wasn't yet ready to give, he considered how to ask the question. "Have you spent any time in small towns?" There. That was safe enough.

"No. Most of my life has been in cities. There were some smaller cities when I was young, but nothing like this."

Not from a small town or village, then. And multiple cities. What sort of life had she led that she'd moved around so often? Military? Clergy's kid? He tucked that tiny piece of her away with his curiosity as he wheeled into the private carpark for the employees of the businesses that lined the high street.

"You ready for this?"

"As ready as I'm going to be."

He believed her. She'd relaxed more over the past couple of days. Having her living situation settled—for now, anyway—had helped. So had the decorating, which was one of the biggest reasons he hadn't blown a gasket about finding all the women in his house and his whole place having been turned upside down. Privately, he could admit to himself that they'd been right. His house was a lot more comfortable and cozy. It just didn't feel like his now. Not in the same way. But that whole interaction seemed to have further relaxed Isobel, so they'd done what they set out to do, and he'd damned well learn to live with it.

The clothes and other supplies they'd ordered online had finally arrived. She still had the borrowed stuff from Ciara, but having her own things had made a difference, too. He'd been curious what the items she'd chosen would say about who she was. Today she'd opted for jeans and some kind of flowy peasant top in a subtle floral pattern. Understated comfort. He wondered if that was an effort to blend in or if this was her norm.

They came in through the back door, straight into the kitchen, where a tall black man with a close-cropped, greying goatee turned from the prep counter. "Ah, good. You're just in time for lunch. We're having cottage pie."

"Lunch?" Isobel whispered. "It's two in the afternoon."

"Aye, but actual lunch is so busy, the staff frequently disnae have time to eat, so Dom makes sure to feed us all once the lunch crowd clears out. Dom, this is Isobel. Isobel, Dominic Bassey. The kitchen is his undisputed domain."

"And don't you forget it." The older man winked to take the sting out of his words. "Go join the others in the back room. I'll be along shortly."

Ewan led her out of the kitchen and down the hall to the back room used for private parties and staff gatherings. The rest of his staff were setting the long table and chatting. They fell silent for two beats as he and Isobel came inside. Then his sister—God love her—beamed. "Isobel! You made it. Welcome."

Isobel edged closer to him and offered a little finger wave. "Hi."

"Everyone, this is Isobel Donnchadh. She's new in town and will be training as a server." He'd already told them yesterday about the basics of her story, so they knew she'd be a bit skittish. He'd wanted to get that part out of the way before he brought her in, so she didn't get self-conscious by having her difficulties—even an abbreviated version of them—mentioned in front of her. Everyone was on board with watching out for her and helping out. "Today she's just going to be here to observe, and we'll probably start formal training tomorrow." He glanced over to see if this was acceptable to her.

Her head bobbed.

His head server, a veteran of this pub long before he'd bought it, set two more plates at the table. "I'm Laura Craig. I'll be the one training you."

Ciara swung an arm around the bony shoulders of the teen boy hanging back with ruddy cheeks. "This gangly lad is our dishwasher, Archie Watson. He helps in the kitchen as well."

Archie's blush deepened as he muttered, "Hullo."

"And I'm Zo Bassey, also a server here. Dom's my father." Her smile flashed bright against her dark skin as she stepped forward to offer a hand to Isobel.

"It's lovely to meet all of you. And please, allow me to apologize to all of you in advance because I'm probably going to make a lot of mistakes. I've never waitressed before. But I promise to work hard and do my best to learn."

"I much prefer that to someone who's convinced they know it all," Laura announced.

"We've a few others who aren't on shift yet," Ewan explained. "One more server—Isla Boyd. And Jason MacKinnon, who stands in as bartender when I'm not working myself."

Dom swung through the door. "Make way for lunch."

They scattered, opening space for him to place the casserole dish in the middle of the table.

"Well, don't just stand there. Sit. I'll grab the bread."

Two minutes later, they were all seated, filling plates and glasses. Ewan worked to keep his focus on his food and his people instead of staring at Isobel to make sure she was okay. She sat between him and Ciara, and seemed relaxed enough, watching and listening to everyone else.

Laura forked up a bite of cottage pie. "So, while you'll technically be a server, The Stag's Head is one of those places where everybody pitches in wherever they're needed. We all pull pints and help Dom with pre-service prep—scrubbing potatoes, chopping onions, and the like."

Ewan figured it was time to go over more of the specifics. "We're open Tuesday through Sunday for lunch and dinner, from eleven to ten. Seven on Sundays. We'll work out what your schedule will be once training is finished. Meals are included on top of your wages."

"You'll have to let me know of any particular favorites. I'll make you some." Dom let his accent slip into the cadence of the West Africa of his youth. "You need to put some meat on those bones. Look like you about to blow away."

Zo laughed. "Dad is all about nourishing the soul through food."

Isobel swallowed a bite of the cottage pie. "If everything you cook is this delicious, I don't think putting on a few pounds will be a problem."

Dom's pleased laugh rolled out. He jerked a thumb in Isobel's direction. "I like this girl."

*So do I.* But Ewan kept the thought to himself.

## 7

"I had the fish and chips, not bangers and mash."

Isobel winced. "I'm so sorry. Let me get that swapped out for you."

She carefully picked up the plate and hustled it back to the kitchen, wondering if she'd written the order down wrong or if this was for another table. She'd already done both of those things more than once tonight.

She was a terrible server.

To be fair, she'd only had one day of training, and it was Friday night. The Stag's Head was packed nearly wall-to-wall with families, friends, and couples having a night out in one of the few venues in town. The noise of boisterous conversation bounced off the rafters, seeming to amplify by the minute. Every time the door opened, she tensed, staring until she was sure it wasn't Paul stepping inside. Then there were the customers. Being a small village, everybody knew the existing servers. She was a fresh face, and everyone wanted to know who she was.

Oh, none of their questions were improper. Just natural curiosity. But she hadn't been prepared for that level of nosiness and the evasive mental maneuvers it would require. She was already exhausted and not even half-way through her shift.

Her respect for waitstaff had magnified exponentially. Keeping orders straight, remembering which tables had requested what, and just carrying things to and fro was *hard*. Like anything else, she assumed she'd get better with practice, but who knew whether Ewan or the rest of his staff could be patient enough for her to learn?

"Dom, I need a fish and chips, please."

"What table?"

"Um... four? Or maybe seven?" Damn it. She couldn't keep them straight, and there was no number *on* the tables.

His kind face softened, even as he moved like a man with eight arms, sliding fish into hot oil and prepping a plate. "No worries. We'll sort it."

Swinging out of the kitchen, she spotted the tray of drinks meant to go to that family of six in the corner. With great care, she lifted it to her shoulder the way Laura had taught her and began to cross the room. *Please don't drop it. Please don't drop it. Please don't drop it.*

Glasses clinked together as the tray shook from her strain and nerves.

*Nearly there.*

A chair bumped her from the side as a patron shoved back from his table. Isobel managed only a squeak as the whole tray shifted and crashed to the floor. Glass shattered and liquid spewed everywhere. The pub went silent, other than the faint murmur of the football game on the TVs in the corners. All she could do was stare in horror at the mess she'd caused.

"Oi! What the bloody hell is wrong with you?"

She flinched back from the angry voice. The patron who'd bumped into her had ended up with most of a beer down his back. He loomed over her, glaring.

Isobel couldn't even manage to babble an apology. Tears welled in her eyes, and her throat had knotted up.

The man took a step toward her, invading her personal space. "I said—"

His words were cut off as a thick, muscular arm propelled him back.

With Ewan's bulk suddenly between them, Isobel could breathe again.

"Tom, your meal is on the house, and I'll pull you another pint if you'll calm the fuck down. If you don't, you're out. I'll not have you abusing my waitstaff."

The two of them stared at each other for only a few seconds before Tom backed down, his own shoulders lowering. "Aye. Right. Can I get a towel?"

"I'll see to it. And for fuck's sake, watch where you're going. You're the one who bumped into her."

As Tom disappeared into the men's room and Ewan went to grab a towel from the bar, conversation started up again. Isobel crouched and began to gather up shards of broken glass, piling them on the tray. She needed a broom and towels. Maybe a mop. No one had told her where any of that was, so she just kept picking up chunks of glassware because she couldn't bear to look at anyone, and she had to do *something*.

"What is this?" At Ewan's bark, her shoulders hunched, her breath clogging in her throat.

But his touch was gentle as he raised her to her feet, turning her hand over. "You cut yourself."

She blinked down at the gash along her pointer finger, which began to well more blood as she stared. "Oh."

Laura and Zo bustled up with the broom and mop.

Laura hissed at the blood. "Ouch! Go get that cleaned up, so it disnae get infected. We'll take care of this."

Ewan nudged her into motion, steering her with a light hand on the small of her back toward the hallway that led to the kitchen and beyond to a room she hadn't seen before. He used a key to unlock it and let them inside what turned out to be a small office. The whole space was occupied by a battered wooden desk, two chairs, and a filing cabinet. He shut the door behind them and pressed her into one of the chairs. She said nothing as he rummaged in the cabinet and came back with a first aid kit, dropping into the chair opposite her.

"Hand."

Isobel extended it, and he began to clean the wound.

"This might hurt a wee bit." He poured disinfectant on the cut, and she grimaced at the sting.

Ewan lifted her hand and blew on it. Gooseflesh erupted all the way up her arm, and she resisted the urge to pull away. Awareness of his touch danced along her skin. She thought again to the night he'd rescued her, to the careful, competent way he'd treated those injuries. Would he ever touch her without blood or bodily harm being involved?

"How's your heid? Are you dizzy? Having headaches? Maybe we started this too soon. It's only been a week since the accident."

She swallowed. "It's kind of you to come up with all those excuses. I think I'm just really bad at this."

Maybe she could find some kind of job as a shop clerk? Or answering phones? It seemed she wasn't suited to anything more complicated.

"You'll learn. Everybody's got to start somewhere." He pressed a gauze pad to the wound and held it to staunch the bleeding.

"I understand if you need to deduct the cost of the glasses or whatever from my pay."

His brows drew down in a scowl, and he made a deep noise of derision in the back of his throat. "Dinna be daft. Broken glassware and crockery is part of doing business. I'm more worried about whether you're okay." He lifted his gaze to hers. The softness there didn't match the gruff tone.

He cradled her wounded hand in his, and his thumb brushed gently back and forth over her palm. Isobel didn't think he realized what he was doing, but it felt incredible. Unable to resist, she curled her hand around his and basked in the sense of connection and kindness. Ewan stilled, and the air between them went thick.

The door swung open. Isobel jolted so hard, she nearly yanked her hand free, but Ewan's grip held her—and the gauze —in place. He reached for a plaster.

Laura stuck her head inside. "Poor little lamb. Everything is fine. Tom's sorted. The mess is cleaned up. Nobody's upset."

She squeezed Isobel's shoulder, and her throat went tight again.

As Ewan continued with the bandage job, Laura eased one hip onto the edge of the desk. "Dinna feel bad, lass. My first waitressing job, I spilled an entire pot of coffee on someone's lap. Followed by the pitcher of water I was carrying because I was terrified I'd scalded her. In the grand scheme of things, a few glasses and some needed laundry are nothing."

"Thank you."

Plaster applied, Ewan released her. Isobel flexed her hand, not because it hurt, but because she wanted to memorize how his skin had felt against hers.

Laura nodded. "You'll learn. But maybe for the rest of tonight, we give you a bit of a break. You can take orders, and we'll deliver them. Your wrist is probably still a mite sore. Ewan said you'd sprained it."

Dom squeezed his way into the crowded little room as well. "If you don't need her out on the floor, I could use a hand in the kitchen scrubbing up some potatoes. Young Archie had to go tend his nan. She had a fall."

Ewan frowned. "Is she okay?"

"Oh, aye. He's gone to make sure she actually rests, as the doctor told her."

They were all just so kind and *nice*. How had she landed in a place with people like this? Or maybe kind people were more common than she'd realized. Perhaps they'd just been chased off or blocked by Paul.

Dom's kitchen seemed a safer option all around. Away from curious eyes.

"Scrubbing potatoes sounds good." Isobel shoved to her feet. "I don't think I can screw that up."

"Then come along, lass. I'll show you how to use the machine that cuts the chips. All you need to do is scrub them up and toss them in..."

FROM HIS POSITION at the end of the bar, Ewan watched Isobel carefully fill drink orders, focusing on the task as if the fate of the world depended on her not spilling a drop. The others would deliver them, for now. She'd ended up out here after taking a half hour to help Dom in the kitchen, which seemed to have restored her equilibrium. Mostly.

Ewan regretted that her first real night had been a Friday, when they were absolutely slammed. He should've started her slower, with the lunch crowd, so she could get used to the process, because she'd spoken nothing but the absolute truth when she'd said she had no experience. Her posture drooped, betraying her exhaustion. But she'd done everything they'd thrown at her without a word of complaint. That was more than he could say for his own sister when she'd been new.

By nine, he was ready to chase the last patrons out himself. He wanted to bundle Isobel home, get her to sit down and rest. But he held his tongue, both because he didn't want to get the village gossip vine started any sooner than it inevitably would by giving his new waitress obvious preferential treatment, and because he understood she needed to end the night on a higher note than it had begun. So it was Laura who shooed the final customer out the front door and locked it at two past ten.

She slumped back against the door. "Whew. Was it a full moon, and I missed it? They were right crazy tonight."

Zo pressed both hands to her lower back and arched until her spine audibly cracked. "I dinna think so, but clearly there was something in the water. I'm for cleaning up and getting home. I have a hot date with my pillow."

Ciara skirted around the bar, nabbing shot glasses. "I'm for all that. But first, we're celebrating Isobel's survival of her first night, which was truly trial by fire."

"Oh." Isobel covered her face with her hands. "I don't know if tonight counts as surviving."

Ewan grabbed a bottle of whisky off the top shelf. "Take the win, lass."

"At the very least, take the shot," Laura urged. "It'll numb the rest."

He poured shots for all of them, including Dom, who emerged from the kitchen.

Ciara was the first to raise her glass. "To Isobel. Welcome to family."

Isobel stared at her for a moment, a stunned expression on her face that melted into a flush as everyone else echoed the sentiment and tossed back their shots. The "Thanks" she uttered before tossing back her own shot was thick with suppressed emotion. Ewan thought of what she'd said about her mother dying when she'd been young. When was the last time she'd had a family, even one so ragtag as the one centered around his pub?

After the toast, his staff scattered, automatically falling into their habitual closing-time routine. Isobel yawned, her jaw stretching wide.

Ewan resisted the urge to touch her again. "Sit down a minute."

"I can sweep. Or wipe down tables. If I'm going to work here, I need to learn how to do everything." The declaration was interrupted by another yawn. But she scooted out from behind the bar to ask Laura what she could do.

Because everyone was motivated, they'd finished wiping down tables, flipping up chairs, and cleaning the floors by half past ten.

Zo put the broom back in the closet. "Tonight, I'm envious of your commute, Ciara."

When Isobel looked baffled, his sister explained, "I live above the pub. I only need climb the back stairs and fall face-first into bed."

At the mention of bed, Isobel yawned again. "I second Zo's envy."

"C'mon. I'll drive you home." So far, only Ciara was aware that was his place. Ewan intended to keep it that way for as long as possible, because their living arrangement would inevitably lead to speculation about the degree of their involvement. Isobel didn't need that additional stress, and he didn't want to deal with the questions.

Because she was listing a little as she walked, he gave in to instinct and took her elbow to steer her back toward the carpark. She didn't jolt at the touch, and he called that a win. Her skin was soft against his, and as they walked, he thought back to that moment in his office, when he'd held her hand in his. To that moment when she'd curled her fingers around his in a connection that he couldn't deny.

There was something between them. Ewan didn't think it was just a matter of closeness because of the situation they found themselves in. They had chemistry. Which didn't matter one bloody bit, because it was still a terrible idea. She was vulnerable. The look on her face when she'd dropped those glasses and Tom had been arsehole had been proof enough of that. She hadn't cowered, but she'd definitely flinched and braced herself for some kind of blow. Infuriated that he could do nothing about what she'd already endured, Ewan had barely restrained himself from physically tossing Tom out on his arse.

He'd done only the necessary. Isobel would have to learn to handle customers on her own. Certainly Laura, Zo, and Ciara all had. It was part of the job. But he'd continue stepping in, if needed, until she got used to it. He didn't really want to analyze his overwhelming urge to not just protect Isobel, but to take care of her, because it was more than clear no one had in a very long time. At the end of the day, he was her protection, and he wouldn't do anything to jeopardize that for her.

They didn't speak on the walk to his Land Rover. Tired as she was, he expected her to be asleep before they'd left the village proper.

Instead, after a few minutes, she murmured, "I know tonight was a little rough. I promise I'm going to work hard. I'll get better."

"As Ciara said, this was trial by fire. Not deliberately, but Friday and Saturday nights are our busiest nights. So the fact that you did as well as you did, in the midst of all that chaos, with zero waitressing experience before, was pretty good."

She glanced over, and he could sense her tired amusement. "I'm pretty sure you're lying, but I thank you for the effort."

They lapsed back into silence for the rest of the drive. Back at the house, they let an ecstatic Havoc out to do his business, and Isobel stumbled toward her room.

"Did you eat tonight?" Ewan asked.

"Dom... made me something." The statement was interrupted by another monstrous yawn.

"Okay. Go on to bed. You're dead on your feet. I'll finish dealing with himself."

"Night."

Her door was closed by the time he and Havoc came back inside from doing his business. Ewan gave the dog his evening biscuit. "Ready for bed?"

Havoc chomped the biscuit in two bites and made a beeline down the hall, nosing at Isobel's door. Apparently, she hadn't shut it all the way because it inched open, and his dog disappeared inside.

Ewan swore and went to retrieve him.

Isobel was already asleep, dark hair spread across her pillow. His traitorous dog was curled up at the foot of the bed, his head resting over her legs.

Well, if that big galumph hadn't woken her when he'd jumped up to join her, maybe Ewan ought to let him stay. Leaving the door ajar so Havoc could get out if he wanted, Ewan headed to his own room to crash.

And if he was jealous of his dog's sleeping arrangements for the night, there was no one awake to judge him.

## 8

After so many years spent touring, Isobel loved having a stable routine. There'd been a sort of routine on the road: traveling from city to city, checking into hotels, running soundchecks, rehearsing, being made up and dressed by costuming, performing, doing press junkets, then packing up and doing it all over again.

But that was absolutely nothing like her life in Glenlaig. After more than two weeks with Ewan, no one had shown up looking for her. Nobody had approached her at the pub to say, "Hey, you look a lot like that violinist who disappeared." Actually, she didn't even know what was being said about her. She still hadn't looked. Isobel knew it was tantamount to believing that if she didn't actually *see* the monster in the closet, it didn't exist. But she was starting to relax and breathe for the first time in longer than she could remember, and she didn't want to rock the boat.

She and Ewan were necessarily on the same schedule, as he was her transportation to and from work. If they also spent most of their downtime together, cooking, reading, and walking the dog, well, Isobel wasn't going to complain. Even if it was more about him playing bodyguard than something more.

He hadn't touched her again. Not since the night he'd bandaged her hand. She'd thought, in the moment, that something had shifted. That this attraction she felt wasn't one-sided. But clearly, she'd misread the vibe of that interaction. He'd been completely professional and friendly. Just her roommate and boss. Her big, brooding, watchful, protective roommate and boss. The one she'd started having naked dreams about.

Was it any wonder when he'd showed up to rescue her in the middle of a storm like some sort of modern knight? He was the stuff of fantasies. Well, maybe he was gruffer and rougher around the edges than any of her prior fantasies, but that just made his deliberate gentleness toward her more apparent and appealing. The care he took with her made Isobel feel... tended. Protected. Seen.

When was the last time anyone had made her feel like that? Never as an adult.

So, if she was harboring a massive crush on her rescuer, she'd decided that was fine. It was something normal. She'd had little enough normal in her world. If he never returned the feeling, that was okay, too. The attraction would run its course, eventually.

*But it is not this day.*

Isobel watched the flex of his muscles as he swapped out one of the kegs on tap. She well knew he could handle her with as much ease. When that led to thoughts of being tossed over those massive shoulders, Isobel shook herself and turned away before she did something really embarrassing, like drool.

Laura stood near the kitchen door, eyes sparkling, her tongue tucked firmly in cheek. "Admiring the view, are we?"

Heat flooded Isobel's cheeks.

"Och, dinna fash yourself. It's a view well worth admiring."

"Well." What could she say to that?

"Order's up in the kitchen."

Relieved to have a task, Isobel escaped into Dom's domain.

He glanced up from the grill and flashed a grin. "Last shift before payday. Big plans tomorrow?"

"I've no idea."

Tomorrow was technically her second Monday off. The first had been spent largely unconscious, recovering from the gauntlet of training through a weekend. She didn't know what she'd do with her wages and the tips she'd managed to earn. Practicality told her to squirrel it all away. Pride had her wanting to offer part of it to Ewan for rent, but when she'd tried to bring it up, he'd gotten all scowly and insulted about it. Another part, the part that had been kept on a leash for far too long, wanted to buy something frivolous, just for her. But that was a decision for later. There was still time left on the clock tonight.

She eyed the order waiting on the counter. "Table six?"

"Aye."

Table six was a group of four. Isobel knew she could carry plates out two at a time. That was how she'd managed the first few days, as it had been safer. She had a lot of wiry strength in her arms from all those years of playing violin, but that was a completely different thing from carting heavy trays of food and drink. Ciara, Zo, and Laura had all offered her suggestions for how to make it easier, and she'd gotten a bit better with practice. To a great extent, it was simply building up her muscle mass for this sort of labor.

Carefully hefting the tray to her shoulder, she tightened her core and began to walk. Archie held the kitchen door open for her, and she flashed him a grateful smile. Eyes scanning her path, she moved slowly but surely through the pub. It was less busy for Sunday evening dinner, so there were fewer patrons to avoid. At table six, she stopped, shifting to slowly grab the first plate from the tray and transfer it to the table. Everyone seemed to hold their collective breath as she eased around the group, delivering their meals. When the last plate made it safely to the table, a minor cheer rang out around the pub. There was no tone of derision. Everyone seemed legitimately proud that she'd pulled it off.

Basking in a sense of achievement, she offered a good-natured bow. "Thank you. Thank you. I'll be here all night."

Grinning as everybody chuckled, she turned back to her customers. "Can I get you anything else? Brown sauce? Mustard?"

The front door of the pub opened, and Isobel tensed, whipping her head in that direction. But it wasn't Paul. It was never Paul. Maybe, eventually, she'd get that through her skull.

Her self-recrimination fell away as she recognized Sophie, Charlotte, and Kyla making their way inside. They spotted her and waved. She waved back and turned her focus to table six again. "I'm so sorry. Was that all?"

Assured that it was, she made a circuit of the room to check her other tables, refilling drinks before making her way over to the women, who'd taken a seat in her section.

Charlotte offered a wide smile. "Hey, Sugar. How's everything going?"

It was nice to see people she... well, didn't exactly *know,* but who she was friendly with. These women had gone out of their way to make sure she was comfortable in her home, no matter how temporary that setup might ultimately be.

"I'd say it's going well. It's been a whole week since I broke a glass or plate." Realizing she'd probably cursed herself, she knocked on the table.

Ciara swung an arm around her shoulders. "She's getting the hang of it. A quick study, she is. Another month and you won't know she hasn't been doing this for ages."

"I appreciate the vote of confidence." Isobel pointedly

pulled out her order pad and pencil. "Can I take your drink orders?"

"Fizzy juice all around," Sophie announced. "We're foregoing alcohol in solidarity."

Kyla folded a hand over the baby belly. "I told you, you dinna have to do that."

"We do not require alcohol to have fun on girls' night," Charlotte insisted.

"Three fizzy juices. Got it. I'll be back in just a few."

Leaving Ciara to visit with her cousin and friends, Isobel went to the bar to put in the drink order. Ewan was building a pint.

"Three fizzy juices for your cousin, Sophie, and Charlotte."

He just nodded and pulled out three glasses with his free hand as he passed the Guinness to an older gentleman perched at the far end of the bar. In less than a minute, he'd loaded the glasses onto her tray. "Just a couple more hours."

"And thank God for it. I'm claiming first dibs on the bathroom when we get home. I want to have a soak."

Something flared in his eyes at the mention of the bath but was gone so fast, Isobel wasn't sure what she'd seen. Maybe surprise that she'd mentioned their living arrangement in public. They'd made it a point to keep that quiet, and she'd forgotten. He definitely wasn't imagining her naked. More was the pity.

Refusing to be weird about it, she lifted the tray and navigated back to the table.

"...if you're going to be there for family dinner on Tuesday?" Kyla was asking. "Angus and Munro will be home."

"Finally!" Ciara crowed. "I wouldn't miss it."

The women's gaze swung to Isobel as she passed out drinks.

"You should come, Isobel," Sophie suggested.

"To what?"

"We have this round robin dinner for our odd little found

family," Charlotte explained. "We bounce back and forth between Lochmara and Ardinmuir, taking turns hosting. This week, we're out at Lochmara."

"Oh, I couldn't intrude."

Kyla waved that away. "Nonsense. My great uncle and his beau are home, and you'll love them. Everyone does. Angus has been off competing in the latest season of *The Great British Bake Off* and is just back. It's guaranteed the desserts will be outstanding."

"True story," Ciara agreed. "Say you'll come."

Something warm lodged itself in her chest at the idea of being included in such a thing. These people were reaching out. Trying to make connections. It was what she wanted, wasn't it?

"Well, if you're sure it's no trouble, I'd love to come. What can I bring?"

"You ken you dinna actually have to bring anything, aye?"

Ewan wasn't sure what he'd expected Isobel to want to do on her day off, but having a wander of the village and picking up groceries wasn't it. That she didn't want to stay holed up at home was a positive step and proved—he hoped—that she was getting more comfortable. He wanted her to feel safe. More, he wanted her to put down some roots. Here. Where he could keep an eye on her and make sure she was okay. Where there were others he trusted who would do the same. Maybe that was completely insane, considering who she was. But she deserved that, if it was something she wanted for herself.

It was nothing at all to do with how his house felt like a home since she'd come into it.

From the passenger seat, Isobel fixed him with a flat stare. "I am not showing up empty-handed to that dinner. My mother taught me better than that."

Understanding this was a line for her, Ewan backed down. It was kind of interesting to see her dig in her heels on something. He hoped that, too, was a sign she was getting more comfortable. She'd disagreed with him without some fear of reprisal.

Shifting in her seat, she crossed her legs, drawing attention to the sundress she wore.

Ewan couldn't quite stop himself from shooting little glances in her direction, noting how the flirty hem exposed several inches of creamy thigh. This had to be one of the loaners from his sister. It definitely hadn't been among the clothes they'd used his credit card to order online. And it was driving him crazy, thinking about what else was underneath that little skirt as he drove into the village. He did not need to be having such thoughts about his roommate. Or his employee. Or the woman he was protecting. But the butter yellow dress with little flowers was so different from the jeans and casual tops she wore to work, and it made her look like walking sunshine. Which made it really hard to remember that whole list of reasons why he was keeping his hands to himself.

At least she'd paired it with a little jumper to counter the still cool temperatures.

Because he could, he parked his 4x4 in the same carpark as he did for work and pocketed the keys. "Okay, you're running the show here. Where would you like to go?"

"Can we just walk a bit? See what's here?"

"It'll be a short walk. But sure."

He fell into step beside her, automatically putting himself on the street side as they strolled down the high street. Her head stayed on a swivel, but from eagerness rather than a place of fear. They passed the pub where it sat on the corner, edging past the chemist and post office, bypassing the estate agent's office with its listings highlighted in the window. Village Chippy wasn't open yet, but he spotted Ryan Beattie inside, already prepping for lunch. The salon at the opposite end was doing a brisk business. Several faces inside turned in their direction, and Ewan had to fight not to wrap an arm around Isobel's shoulders to shield her from view. That would be sure to get the gossip mill churning. She hesitated at the newsagent and convenience store on the corner, but ultimately moved on.

"Is there anything down this street?"

"It's largely residential, but there's the library. It's wee, but surprisingly well stocked."

She brightened at that. Then her face fell. "I can't get a library card without ID."

He didn't point out that she did have ID in her wallet. He'd seen it for himself that first night. But it didn't carry the name she'd given everyone, so he held his tongue. "We can work on that. And either way, I've got an account. I can check things out for you."

But she turned away to cross the street. "Another time. You have a surprisingly nice collection at the house yourself. Why is that, by the way? I don't think I've met any other guys who read romance."

Ewan shrugged. He knew that didn't fit with anyone's image of who he was. "It's encouraged in the military. Romance is all about hope. When we're out on deployment in one shitehole or another, that's often in short supply. That was how I got started. My mum and Ciara both love them and were happy to bring me more."

"You have a good relationship with your mum?"

"Aye, good enough. She has a tendency to try to smother me now that I've retired. But we get on. Da, too."

"Do they live here in Glenlaig?"

"They do. Though they've been on a long holiday around the Mediterranean, which is why they havenae been beating my door down to meet you." That reprieve would end soon. Ciara might stay quiet, but no way would the rest of the village. His mother would hear about Isobel within five minutes of getting home. And that was assuming nobody emailed her in the meantime. He wasn't looking forward to that. She'd have questions, and he still didn't have all the answers. Plus, she'd take the fact that he'd moved Isobel into his house as tantamount to an engagement. He really needed to figure out what he was going to say about that before she put Isobel in an uncomfortable position.

"Oh!" Isobel darted toward the door of the little visitor's center.

Ewan had no idea what had caught her eye, but dutifully followed her inside. The place was full of souvenirs and maps, generally catering to the steady stream of tourists they got during the warmer months. Jeanne Clarke, the owner, also offered booking services for tours and various outdoor excursions in the area. He hadn't ever had a reason to go inside before.

Isobel went straight to a display of wind chimes, reaching up to gently set the center string swaying. As the chimes rang out, her face lit up with pure joy. "Oh, that's lovely. Such a clear tone. We had wind chimes on the balcony of our flat when I was wee. My father and I used to sit out there, listening to the music of the wind for hours."

It was the first truly personal thing she'd told him, and Ewan added it to that puzzle in his head, even as he watched her close her eyes and listen, her fingers twitching to each bell-like tone, until the last note died away. Her sigh told him it was a good memory, but after one glance at the price, she kept moving, wandering the other racks and displays.

He supposed it made sense. Despite all the help he'd provided, she was starting over and on a limited budget. And wind chimes were a thing you bought for your home. Maybe she didn't feel comfortable enough at his place to buy such a thing. Or maybe she didn't plan on staying.

*Dinna be daft. She disnae know* what *she's doing yet. It's her choice to buy it or not buy it.*

Abandoning the display, he joined her as she browsed.

At the display of silver jewelry, she lingered, examining the triquetras, the triskelions, the shield knots, and other Celtic symbols, pausing to read the descriptions on each of the little cards. It was a thistle pendant she ultimately chose. He didn't miss the description that it represented overcoming adversity and difficult situations. Definitely appropriate.

Necklace clutched in her hand, she turned toward the checkout. "Oh! They have an ice cream counter in the back!"

"Do you like ice cream?"

"Mmm, love it. But I'm not allowed." The words fell from her mouth in the way of an oft-repeated statement.

Ewan could only stare. What kind of grown adult wasn't allowed to have ice cream? Maybe it was a health thing? "Are you diabetic? Allergic?"

"No."

Furious at the remaining implication, he made a decision on the spot. "Then you're having some."

"Ewan, it's ten in the morning."

"So? Would you like ice cream?"

"I mean yes, but—"

"Then you'll have some." Needing to give her *something*, he nudged her toward the back, where Jeanne was waiting at the counter.

"What can I get you today?"

Isobel studied the flavors on offer. "It's hard to choose. They all look delicious!"

"All local and freshly made on-site. My personal favorite is butter pecan. But the chocolate chocolate chunk is delicious as well."

"Actually, I think I'd like to try the caramel apple cobbler."

"I'll get you a sample." Opening the cooler, Jeanne loaded up the tip of a wee wooden spoon and handed it over.

Isobel took it, her pink lips closing around it with a faint moan that went straight to Ewan's crotch. "Oh, yes. That one, for sure. A scoop of that."

Grateful for the freedom of his kilt, he shifted his sporran to mask his arousal. "Make hers a double. I'll have one, too."

"I repeat: It's ten in the morning."

"Life is too short no' to have the ice cream."

Her prismatic eyes began to dance, and she laughed. It was the first full, unfettered smile he'd seen from her, and it slammed into his solar plexus like a fist.

"Okay, then. A double scoop."

"Coming right up. Cup or cone?"

"Cup, please."

Ewan sent up a brief prayer of thanks that he wouldn't have to endure watching her lick a cone. His sporran wasn't big enough to hide what *that* would do to him.

When they had their ice cream, Isobel thanked Jeanne and him again, and paid for her necklace. Then she wandered toward the front of the shop. Ewan hung back.

"Havenae seen you smile like that since before you left for the military," Jeanne murmured.

Self-conscious, Ewan wiped the smile right off his face. "Aye, well. Thanks for the ice cream."

"Any time."

Checking to see that Isobel was out of earshot, he lowered his voice further. "Did you see the wind chimes she was admiring when we came in?"

"I did."

"Set it aside. I'll be back to get it later." He knew this would get the gossips going, but he just couldn't help himself.

Jeanne grinned. "I'll make it so."

## 9

Nerves jittered in Isobel's stomach, and tonight she wouldn't be able to lose them in making music. The lack of it ached like the pulse of a phantom limb. But she shoved that aside and surreptitiously wiped her hands on her trousers. She wasn't afraid. Not like she had been. But she needed to make a good impression. These people were the closest thing she'd had to friends in... well, years, and she wanted them to like her.

Clutching the plastic container, she followed Ewan up to a rear door of the manor house at Lochmara, vaguely horrified when he just walked in without knocking. Then again, Ciara had done the same at his house, so maybe they were all that kind of easy with each other. The door led into the kitchen, which was something of a madhouse, with people standing everywhere and the black and white dog she'd seen on her last visit making a sneaky attempt to snatch something off the counter.

Charlotte leapt forward to save the platter. "Dugal! Down. Not yours. Raleigh put him outside. I swear..." She turned and spotted them. "Isobel! Ewan! Welcome. You're just in time.

We're about five minutes out from supper. What have you got there?"

Ewan held up his six-pack of beer, even as Isobel tightened her fingers on the container.

"It's just a wee appetizer."

With cheerful efficiency, Ciara sidled up and plucked it from her fingers. "I'll add it to the spread." She cracked the top and crowed. "Oh! Smoked salmon. I love smoked salmon." Popping one of the skewers with cream cheese and cucumber into her mouth, she hummed a happy note and shot Isobel a thumbs up.

Well, at least one person liked them.

Kyla waddled over, long red hair pulled back into a curling tail, one hand on her baby belly. "Welcome. You remember my husband Raleigh, and Malcolm and Gavin." Isobel nodded greetings as she continued, gesturing to a tall blond man trying to steal one of the salmon skewers from Ciara, who danced out of reach. "And this is my brother, Connor."

"Guilty."

Because it seemed polite, Isobel nodded at him. "Congratulations on your engagement."

Connor's face lit up like a beacon. "Thanks!"

Ewan passed him one of the beers. "I dinna ken what she sees in you, Cousin, but I'm happy for you both just the same."

"I dinna ken either, but I plan to worship her for the rest of her life, so she disnae throw me back."

Isobel looked around for the woman in question. "Where is Sophie?"

"Putting together the flowers for the table," Kyla explained. She circled around the counter and looped her arm through that of an older gentleman with a shock of white hair and bright blue eyes that matched hers. "And this is my great uncle Angus, whom we all adore. And his partner Munro Sinclair."

Angus's eyes twinkled as he pressed a kiss to Kyla's cheek. "I adore you right back, my wee lass."

She laughed. "Not so wee anymore."

"The bairn will come soon enough. I'm just glad we didnae miss it."

Munro, a tall, slim man with olive skin and silver hair, looked on with amusement. "It was all he could talk about in Berkshire, other than baking."

"Well, I wasnae allowed to talk about the show now, was I?"

"I still canna believe you won't tell us *any*thing," Ciara pouted.

"Them's the rules," Angus intoned.

The door opened again, and another man strode in, accompanied by a willowy young girl Isobel pegged around twelve years old. "Sorry we're late. Everything's still in boxes, but herself insisted we had to bring something."

Isobel met Ewan's gaze and arched her brows. *See?*

Charlotte took what appeared to be a box of digestive biscuits from him. "These will go just fine with after dinner tea and coffee."

Kyla continued introductions. "Hamish, we'd like you to meet Isobel Donnchadh, Glenlaig's newest resident. Isobel, our dear friend Hamish Colquhoun and his daughter Freya. They've just moved back to Glenlaig."

She waggled her fingers. "Hullo."

Hamish nodded a greeting, his sharp eyes shifting between her and Ewan, who'd materialized at her side like a ghost. It was clear the other man had questions, but he didn't give voice to any.

Charlotte clapped her hands. "Freya, why don't you and Gavin finish setting the table? We'll start dishing everything up."

The girl's cheeks colored at the request. She darted a sidelong look at Gavin before following him out of the room.

Connor crossed to Hamish and pulled him in for a back-thumping hug. "How are things on the divorce front?"

"Final. Thank God."

"We'll all drink to that tonight."

"How's Freya taking the move?" Raleigh asked.

Hamish combed a hand through his thick, dark hair. "Good, so far. My parents are spoiling her something fierce, and it's feeling like we'll never be unpacked, so I dinna think she's had time to really process everything."

"Give her time, mate. She'll be all right," Connor assured him.

As if responding to some silent signal, everyone leapt into motion, beginning to transfer food to serving bowls and grabbing up dishes and baskets. Ill at ease, and with nothing to occupy her hands, Isobel hung back, not sure what to do.

Munro appeared at her elbow. "This lot has everything well in hand. How about you and I select some music for the meal?"

Grateful for the save, she smiled at him. "That would be lovely."

She trailed him into the dining room, waiting as he paired his phone with the Bluetooth speaker there and pulled up an internet radio app.

"Do you have a preference?"

A thousand options popped into her head. Pieces she'd been playing in her mind for the past two weeks. But she deliberately kept her suggestions vague. "For ambiance, something instrumental, I think. Classical? Jazz? Maybe a film score?"

"Have a favorite composer?"

"For old school, Elgar."

"That's as good a start for a new station as any." He tapped in the name and hit play.

The opening strains of the orchestral version of Edward Elgar's *Salut d'amour* poured from the speaker. Her fingers reflexively twitched the fingering of the notes, her brain latching on to something familiar and wanting to run with it. But before she could sink into it and lose herself, Ewan appeared, nudging her toward one side of the table that was now loaded with food.

She ended up between him and Ciara. Everyone began passing platters and bowls, talking over each other. Her attention automatically turned back to the music, which had shifted into "The Swan" from Camille Saint-Saëns' *Carnival of the Animals*. The rise and fall of the strings was moody and tugged at her heart, as it always did, filling her up, until she ached with the need to pick up her instrument and pour out the overflow of emotion.

A strong, warm hand encircled hers beneath the table even as Ciara's quiet voice sounded in her ear. "—you all right?"

Isobel blinked, realizing she'd closed her eyes and pressed a hand to the tightness in her chest. "What?"

Ciara's brows were knit with concern. "You're crying."

Isobel felt the tension vibrating through Ewan's frame even before she looked in his direction. His eyes were intense, as if he were ready to do battle with whatever had upset her. Instinctively, she squeezed back, wanting to reassure him.

Echoes of concern sounded around the table.

Heat rushed into her face as she felt more tears roll down her cheeks. Mortified, she wiped the wetness away. "Sorry. It's just... this piece always hits me right in the feels."

Across the table, Munro nodded with understanding. "It's a truly lovely piece. But then Saint-Saëns so often pulls on all the emotional heartstrings."

"Doubly so, as this was my father's favorite. He used to play it for me every night as a lullaby when I was little."

Ewan squeezed her hand again, his thumb brushing over her knuckles in a gesture that was probably meant to be soothing but lit up her nerve endings instead.

"What a cherished memory. Your father clearly had excellent taste in music."

She was grateful Munro had picked up on the past tense and not asked about it. "He did, indeed."

"You never know quite what will remind you of them after they're gone," Kyla said. "Connor and I lost our parents more than a decade ago, and every now and then, something just blindsides me." She offered a wry smile. "More so now that I'm amped up by all the pregnancy hormones."

For a long, humming beat, she held the other woman's gaze, acknowledging that sense of kinship that could only come from mutual experience of loss.

"That's part of why we do these dinners," Charlotte added. "Because all of us here have lost somebody, and we're hanging on to the people we've still got."

Ewan still hadn't released her hand. Was he hanging onto her? God, she hoped so.

Moved by Charlotte's sentiment, Isobel tipped her head in acknowledgment. "Thank you for including me."

Knowing she needed to start eating, she squeezed Ewan's hand once more and picked up her knife to cut the chicken.

Angus entered into the silence. "Well, we're always glad to expand the family."

Something about that had Munro repressing a snort.

Angus shot him a faux glare. "Speaking of expanding the family, it seems as good a time as any to mention... Munro and I eloped in Berkshire."

Everyone exploded.

"What?"

"Holy shite!"

"That's wonderful!"

Connor leapt up from his seat and raced around to hug them both. "It's about bloody time."

Congratulations flowed along with more than one bottle of

champagne and some sparkling apple juice for the expectant mother as toasts were offered to their health and happiness. Through the rest of the meal, the mood was decidedly convivial, with so much enthusiasm and acceptance that Isobel thought she'd be feeling the aftermath of its glow for days.

She might be missing her music, but this was a feeling she hadn't ever found with anywhere else. If it was the tradeoff for walking away from her heart, she thought it just might go a long way toward mending the break.

EWAN EYED HAMISH as he slumped rather than slid onto a stool at the far end of the bar. "Do you need a pint or something stronger?"

"The pint's fine. And some lunch." He rolled his shoulders and cracked his neck.

"Everything okay? Is Dayna being a problem?" Now that the divorce was final, was his ex-wife changing her mind about custody arrangements?

"For once, no. I'm just exhausted. I'm still telecommuting to wrap up my standing caseload in Edinburgh, and between all that, I'm working on the house and updating the building I bought to be my office here. It's just a lot."

"You realize we're all willing to pitch in to help with renovations, aye?"

Hamish just arched a brow. "Because you're so adept at asking for help yourself?"

Ewan's lips twitched as he pulled a pint of Hamish's usual IPA. "We're no' talking about me."

"I appreciate it. And aye, I know that well enough. But right now, the physicality of it is sort of my personal therapy."

"I get that. Still, offer stands."

"Noted. And same goes. You know there's not a soul in this village who wouldn't step up to help if you needed it, aye?"

"Aye. I ken that." He'd just never had cause to test the theory.

Hamish sipped at his beer and sighed. "I needed that." He angled his head, listening. "Did you change the music up?"

Ewan fought the urge to shift on his feet. After he'd seen how much Isobel had enjoyed the music at dinner the other night—her father's favorite notwithstanding—he'd been playing around some with the playlists running in the background at the pub. Today's was centered around orchestral arrangements of popular songs, and several times he'd caught her humming, the fingers of her left hand twitching, as if she were playing them herself. She had to be missing it.

"Just trying something different." Not wanting to acknowledge the knowing look Hamish sent his way, he changed the subject. "Where's Freya today? With your folks?"

"They've been helping out a lot, and are delighted to do it, but they're getting a wee break today, as well. Raleigh's taking her and Gavin out on a trail ride. You'd think she was getting her own horse for how excited she was about it."

Ewan pursed his lips. "You ken she'll probably be asking for one after? Because she's right at that age when wee girls get obsessed with horses. And you bought a house with land and room, so you dinna have a lot of reasons to say no."

Hamish rubbed at the furrow between his brows. "Let me survive the request for a puppy first."

"Just warning you."

"Fair enough. And I want that for her. The whole reason I moved her here was to give her a taste of the kind of childhood we all had. The riding, hiking, and all the adventures we had across the estates."

Ewan's gaze slid across the pub to where Isobel was refilling drinks. From everything she'd said, she hadn't had much of a childhood herself. Maybe he could do something about it now.

She caught his eye as she turned and lifted a brow. He waved her over. He could've taken Hamish's order himself, but she needed the practice. He'd moved them both to the lunch shift this weekend to let her get some more experience under less hectic circumstances.

She skirted behind him at the bar. "Hello, Hamish. Here for some lunch?"

"I am, indeed."

"What can I get you?" Order pad in hand, she waited, confirming what he wanted before carefully writing it down. "I'll get this on back to Dom. It was nice to see you again."

They both watched as she disappeared into the kitchen.

"So, what's the story there?"

Ewan went stone-faced. Her story wasn't his to tell. "I'm just helping her out of a bad situation."

Hamish met his flat stare with the lawyer face that clearly told Ewan he knew there was more to it than that. But he didn't push. "Good of you. If there's anything I can do to help with that, you know I will."

Yeah, he'd already started thinking about that. "Appreciate it."

The rest of the lunch shift went smoothly. Isobel was finally getting the hang of things, having memorized the table layout and the menu. Her tray skills still needed some work, but no one gave her grief about it, and all their meals and drinks were delivered safely, which was what mattered in the end.

Once the crowd had departed and the doors closed for an hour, they all sat down for their own midday meal in the back room.

Isla reached for the bowl of spaghetti Dom had put together for them, dancing a little in her seat. "I dinna ken who took over the radio, but I have to say I fully approve. This is a lovely change from the usual. What is it?"

Isobel had that faraway look she often got listening to music. "Vitamin String Quartet. They specialize in popular covers. They've done a lot of stuff for the *Bridgerton* series."

"Oh, I love the music in that!"

Zo snickered. "It wasnae the music I was paying attention to in season one. Two words: Simon. Bassett."

"You're not wrong," Laura conceded. "But I'm in it for Collin and Penelope. I can't *wait* until he gets his head out of his arse and notices how wonderful she is."

Ewan met Dom's gaze across the table. "Do you ken what the hell they're on about?"

"I've learned it's best not to ask. Have some garlic bread."

"Who are you watching for, Isobel?" Zo prompted.

"Oh, I haven't seen it."

Conversation screeched to a halt as all the women stared at her.

"That's it," Isla announced. "An intervention is needed. Watch party. My place as soon as we can square our schedules."

Ewan waited to see if he needed to wade in, but Isobel only grinned. "That sounds like fun."

The rest of the meal was full of more discussion about must-watch shows. Isobel drifted in and out of the conversation as her attention clearly shifted to the music each time it changed. Laura and Zo were in an impassioned debate about *Ted Lasso* when the song changed yet again. After only a couple of bars, all color leeched from Isobel's cheeks.

She muttered a hurried, "Excuse me," and pushed back from the table.

Dom eyed her with concern as she disappeared into the restroom. "I hope she doesn't have some kind of food allergies she hasn't mentioned."

"I'm sure the food's fine." Surreptitiously, Ewan checked the music app on his phone, wondering if this was another case of memories brought up by the song. Then he spotted the artist. Elizabeth Duncan.

*Ah.* Perhaps changing up the music hadn't been the best idea after all.

She seemed mostly composed when she returned a few minutes later. As everyone began clearing the table, he jerked his head toward the office. "Speak to you for a minute?"

With an about-face, she walked back down the hall.

He shut the door behind them. "Are you okay?"

"Yeah. No, I'm fine." The restless hand she tunneled through her hair belied the words, but he elected not to push directly.

"Look, I feel compelled to mention that Hamish is an attorney. If there are any legal issues around your situation, he can help untangle them, whatever they may be. He's trustworthy, discreet, and verra good at his job."

She bit her lip. "I'll think about it."

He reminded himself of all the reasons he didn't want to push her. She was making progress. He didn't want to mess that up by forcing the issue. They had time.

Instead, he shifted gears. "Do you have plans for your next day off?"

Amusement lit her eyes. "What would I be doing?"

"I dinna ken. You could've made plans with Ciara or that whole watch party thing Isla was talking about."

"I don't have plans, at the moment, no."

"Well, will you spend it with me? I have something I want to show you." He didn't realize how date-like the request sounded until the words were out. That wasn't what this was about.

But interest sharpened her gaze. "Sure. I'd love to."

## 10

"Ever ridden one of these before?"

Isobel eyed the ATV with a mix of giddy anticipation and trepidation. "Definitely not."

Ewan lifted a cooler and a couple of other bags onto the rack mounted at the back and strapped them down with practiced ease. "Normally, I'd just hike in, but you're no' accustomed to that, and you dinna have the right kind of boots. So we'll ride."

There was only one ATV. "Together?"

He paused in the process of strapping a couple of fishing poles down. "Aye. Is that a problem?"

There were clearly foot pegs for a second rider, but to fit, she'd have to be pressed up against his back. That broad, muscular back not remotely hidden by the grey t-shirt he wore. Just the idea of it had her internal temperature rising. "No."

"Then put this on."

She took the helmet he offered and tugged it on, grateful she'd gone for a ponytail this morning. Ewan crouched to check the fit, peering at her through the visor before fastening the chin strap. Apparently satisfied, he nodded, then plucked the other helmet from where he'd set it on the seat and climbed on the machine himself.

"On you go."

With a deep breath, she braced a hand on his shoulder and swung her leg over the seat, dropping behind him like a stone. There were a couple of modest inches between them, but she was still close enough she could feel the heat of him in contrast to the coolness of the morning. She wanted to snuggle up against him and rub her cheek against his back.

*Down, girl.*

He waited until she'd settled with her feet on the pegs before whistling for Havoc. The big dog gave a joyful bark and bounced as if waiting for a starter pistol to fire. The moment Ewan cranked the ATV, he was off like a shot.

"Hold on!"

With a rev of the engine, the machine leapt forward. On a little shriek, Isobel gave up any pretense of distance and grabbed onto Ewan, wrapping her arms around his waist and gripping his hips with her knees as if her life depended on it. A hand settled on her calf and squeezed. She recognized his silent reassurance and eased her hold a little. He wouldn't let anything happen to her.

Pressed against him as she was, she felt each shift of his body as he maneuvered the vehicle. She could also feel the ridges of his abs beneath her palms where they rested on his belly and had to resist the urge to slip her hand beneath his shirt to trace them. The blast of lust distracted her from that initial burst of fear, and Isobel realized they weren't going that fast. Ewan drove as he did everything else—with competence and confidence. The track he followed wound into the trees. Havoc kept pace beside them in an easy, loping run, tongue lolling, eyes bright and happy.

They rode for perhaps half an hour before the land opened

up. Trees gave way to meadow. A burbling stream cut through the center, and hills rolled up on either side, rising into rocky peaks. There was no sign of human habitation. No sign that humans had ever been here at all, save the faded trail they'd followed. They were completely, gloriously alone.

Ewan parked a little way from the stream, at the base of a cluster of wide boulders, and gestured for her to get off.

She did as he asked, removing the helmet and turning a circle, trying to take in everything at once. "This is positively gorgeous. What is this place?"

"It's part of Ardinmuir's estate." He released the straps and began gathering the supplies he'd packed.

"I didn't think we were that close to the castle."

"We're not. They've got about twelve thousand acres. My land and my house actually used to be a part of it. My cousins sold me that parcel when I retired from the Royal Marines. I've got free run of the place. Something I havenae taken advantage of for a while. I used to come out here all the time as a boy."

"Really?" She took the small cooler he passed her and followed when he carried all but one bag up the rocks.

"Aye. We'd hike and camp. Did a lot of horseback riding, too. Back then, Ardinmuir had horses. Those got sold several years ago." He leapt across a gap between the rocks, then held out his hand for hers.

She took it, letting him steady her as she jumped after. "It sounds like a fairly idyllic childhood."

"I didnae think about it at the time, but aye, it was. I ken you didn't get to have a lot of those sorts of experiences yourself, so I thought I'd bring you out here for a taste of it."

Moved by his thoughtfulness, she couldn't resist laying a hand on his arm. "Thank you for that."

Looking uncomfortable with her gratitude, he patted her hand and turned away. "We'll fish for our lunch."

"As you may have guessed, I've never done that before, either. What's the plan if we don't catch anything?"

"There's stuff in the cooler. But this spot always has fish this time of year."

"I'll take your word for it."

The stream flowed into a wide, natural depression, forming a decent sized pool before it flowed on through the rocks. She spotted the flash of silver in the water. Ewan set up the rods and gave her a basic tutorial. He got bonus points for not making her touch the worm. Then they settled in to wait. Bored, Havoc wandered off to investigate.

"Should we call him back?"

"He'll be fine. He kens this area well, and he'll likely turn back up when we start cooking."

The quiet here was profound. They were miles from anything resembling civilization. Freed of the burden of keeping up her awareness, Isobel relaxed and simply listened, soaking in the twitter of birdsong and the whisper of wind through the trees. The gurgle of water over rock added another layer to nature's song, and her mind began to spin, thinking through how she'd translate these sounds, this feeling, into music.

With her head caught up in song, she almost dropped the fishing pole when the hard tug came on the line. "Oh!"

"Grab it! Jerk back hard to set the hook!"

The tip of the rod dipped with tension as she worked to reel in her catch.

"C'mon. C'mon. You've got it!" He knelt at the edge of the rock, a net in hand, ready and waiting when the wriggling fish came out of the water. Scooping beneath it, he brought it in and grinned up at her. "You caught your first fish!"

That unfettered grin punched Isobel right in the gut, and in that moment, she could see shades of the boy he'd once been. "So I did. Is it big enough for lunch?"

"A small one, maybe. But I've got a big appetite. We'll keep going awhile. Unless you're bored?"

"No. No, this is lovely. Peaceful."

He took care of the fish and re-baited her hook. Over the next hour, he began to talk in a low, quiet voice, telling her more about his adventures as a boy. She loved seeing this piece of him and wondered how long it had been since he'd thought of it himself. By the end of it, they'd caught three more fish—one for her, two for him. Her second was too small to keep, so Ewan released it. The rest, he set aside for lunch.

In fascination, she watched him put together a fire that he lit with a flint from his pocket. Then he filleted the fish with a wickedly sharp knife he'd brought, seasoned them with spices from the remaining bag, and set them over the fire to in a wire basket he'd brought. She investigated the contents of the rest of the bag and found tortillas, and a zip-top bag of what looked like cabbage slaw. It was the avocado that clued her in.

"Fish tacos by campfire?"

He flashed that grin again. "Why not?"

"You'll get no complaints from me."

While he cooked, she made herself useful, prepping the tortillas with the slaw and cutting the avocado into chunks. As ever, he didn't press for conversation. The fact that she could be silent with him was a gift unto itself. But after he'd given her a piece of himself, she felt as if she owed him more of her.

"My father's parents didn't approve of my mother."

He lifted his gaze to hers. "No?"

"They never told me why. I suspect at least part of it was that Mum got pregnant with me out of wedlock. I did the math around when they got married and when I was born. I don't know if that's all it was. All they ever told me was that they fell in love, and when his parents didn't support them, he left. So I never knew my dad's family. Mum's family wasn't in the picture either, so it was always just the three of us. We got by. My father was a musician. Not the sort that ever amounts to much in terms of money from performances. But he taught, and between his students and mum's house-cleaning clients we got by."

"He's where you got your love of music."

"Aye. Everything from classical to Celtic to pop and rock. There was nothing he didn't love. When I think of childhood, it's in song. A whole array of memories, underscored with an endless soundtrack. Even now, I walk around most of the time with music playing in my head. For me, music is always joy because it was his."

As the fish was ready, she paused in her tale so they could prepare their plates. Then she settled in beside him and bit in. The bite of lime and the heat of chilis exploded in her mouth in a symphony of taste.

"Mmm, delicious."

For a few minutes, they ate in silence.

Eventually, he set his empty plate aside. "What happened to him? Your father?"

"He got sick. Thought it was nothing. Pushed it aside. Chalked it up to just being tired and working too much. There was a lot going on then." All around her and the life they'd orchestrated to nurture her talent. She swallowed down the lump in her throat. "By the time my mother bullied him into going to the doctor, it was already stage four. Lung cancer, though he'd never smoked. He was gone in less than six months."

"How old were you?"

"Nearly twelve. I was devastated. He understood me better than anyone else. I had some... unusual needs as a child." She supposed that was as good a description as any of being so gifted she'd earned a spot at the Royal Academy of Music that early. "The man who would ultimately become my guardian came into my life because of them. My mother was lost without my father. So when—" Isobel cut herself off before she could utter Paul's name. "—when he showed up offering to help, she jumped at the chance. It wasn't a romantic attachment. And he was good to us both then. For years. Then my mother was killed in a hit-and-run when I was fifteen."

"Jesus."

Because she couldn't dwell on it and not cry, she pushed on. "As there was no family, I was left in his custody. He was the adult in my life. He was the one who made all the calls. And for a long time, it was fine. He took care of me the way he had taken care of both of us when my mother was still alive. It wasn't until I got older that things started to change."

Isobel knew Ewan well enough by now to sense the tension snapping into his body even before she glanced over to see a muscle jumping in that square jaw.

"Did he... try to get physical?"

"No. No, it was never that. Thank God. But the more I started to try to stretch my wings and do what *I* wanted, the more he started to shift and change. It wasn't like a switch got flipped. He was very slick about it, and he did what all abusers ultimately manage to do. He cut me off from anyone who could have been an ally or a friend, who might have pointed out, hey, what he's doing is not okay. We've led a very mobile life, so we weren't in any one place long enough for me to make connections that might have helped get me out."

"What finally made you leave?"

"It was a combination of things. He believes he owns me. I know that doesn't make sense to you. I can't explain it fully right now. But it was that and the fact that he got careless. He'd laid hands on me before, but never rough enough that he left a mark." She rubbed at the phantom ache that flared in her wrist. "It was an escalation, and I was afraid of where that might go, so I managed to slip away and ended up here. For which I am incredibly grateful. I don't like to think about where I'd be if you hadn't found me."

Eyes searching her face, he reached out to tuck a lock of hair behind her ear. "You'd have figured it out. You're incredibly brave."

This man had been so kind, going above and beyond what any reasonable person would've done for a stranger. He'd given her a home and a job and protection. As they sat close enough she could feel him breathing, the air between them felt weighted with things unsaid. There was something here. Something bigger than kindness. He'd said on multiple occasions he didn't want to manipulate her or push her into anything. Was he holding back out of a sense of honor because he believed she was vulnerable? God, she wanted to believe that. Wanted to believe it so much, she decided to be brave again and take a risk.

Before she could over-analyze or think better of it, she closed the distance between them, laying her lips against his. She hadn't kissed many people. There'd been little opportunity over the years. But she knew enough to be aware that the fact that he didn't kiss her back wasn't a good sign.

Heart sinking, she pulled back, murmuring, "Thank you."

She'd play it off as no big deal. She'd just misread the situation. She'd—

"Isobel." His voice had gone to gravel, and his eyes were one step above feral.

Hope was a wild thing in her chest as she took one more risk and leaned in again.

This time he met her halfway, his mouth taking hers in that same confident, competent way he did everything. But she felt him tremble, understood that he was holding back, even as his warm lips played over hers. She framed his face, angling her head to take the kiss deeper. His arms wrapped around her, hauling her closer, until they were pressed chest to chest, heart to thundering heart. Every inch of her lit up with need. How could she feel so alive, so aroused, so wanted, and yet still so safe?

Maybe that was it. He made her feel safe enough to be reckless with him.

With a little whimper, she threaded her fingers in the hair at his nape and pressed closer, wanting to feel that hard, hot body against hers. When he fell back, it felt like a triumph. She shifted to straddle him, feeling the bulge of his arousal between them.

*God, yes.*

A single, happy bark was the only warning she got before a hundred pounds of canine joined in what he apparently thought was a wrestling match. Ewan rolled, putting himself between her and the dog.

He shoved Havoc away. "Get off, you eejit."

An eye-wateringly noxious odor seemed to join the fray. "Oh, God, what is that smell?"

"He's found something to roll in. Go. Go!" With an insulted harumph, the dog walked away to sulk, thankfully somewhere downwind.

When Ewan rolled off her, Isobel nearly sank into a sulk herself.

"Are you alright?"

Her nipples felt like marbles, and she was pretty sure she'd soaked her underwear. She was also pretty sure he'd come to his senses, so no, she wasn't all right.

"I'm not hurt."

He sat up, tunneling both hands through his hair before looking at her. "This isnae a good idea."

She could see him retreating, putting back up those noble walls. But she knew now what was behind them, and she wasn't satisfied with the idea of losing it. "Maybe not. But it doesn't change the fact that this is here. And before your honor rears up to protest, this is not gratitude—although certainly I am grateful to you. It's not hero worship. We're attracted to each other, and we both know it now. So we have to decide what to do about it."

She knew what she wanted to do. She wanted to pursue this. Wanted him naked and over her, under her. Inside her.

Loosing a shuddering breath, he took her hand and pulled her upright. "I think we'd best be verra, verra careful."

Well, it wasn't a denial, and it wasn't a no.

She could work with that.

RESTRAINT WAS GOING to kill Ewan.

It had been two days since the kiss, and it had taken all his considerable control to keep from following through on where that first explosive encounter had been heading. He wasn't fool enough to insult Isobel by suggesting she didn't know her own feelings. But he was still very aware she'd experienced years of trauma because of power dynamics, and he didn't want to do anything to inadvertently pressure her, no matter how attracted he was. And damn it, he couldn't stop thinking about how she tasted, how she felt in his arms, wrapped around him. A high-definition reel of it had been playing on repeat in his head, accompanying him into the shower. Into his dreams.

He wanted her in a way he hadn't wanted anyone or anything since he'd left for basic training, determined to become the best of the best. But they had to take it slow. Not only because it was in her best interest, but because it was in his. This whole domestic partnership they'd fallen into at home had done nothing but fuel his fantasies of her staying and becoming a part of the fabric of his life here, and that wasn't fair to her.

Though he'd stuck to his decision not to read the full

dossier Conroy had prepared, he'd filled in some blanks from the story she'd told about her childhood and the death of her parents. While she hadn't spelled it out, he was guessing the former guardian was her manager, Paul Burgette. Or was he her agent? Both? Ewan supposed it didn't matter. He likely had control over her career. That had to be what she'd meant by him thinking he owned her. The bastard.

Eventually, Isobel would have to face her past and everything she'd walked away from. Ewan would do whatever was necessary to help get her untangled from that situation. And then what? Though he didn't know all the particulars, Conroy had let drop some details about her album sales that suggested she was a big fucking deal. What were the chances that, once she was free, she'd want to walk away from the life she'd led to live in his tiny village working in his pub for any kind of long-term? It had been easier for him to imagine that in the beginning, before he knew anything about who she was.

And yet...

She needed a home. A family. Some normal. She was starving for it. She could have all that here, with him. She *did* have all that here, for now.

Across the pub, she laughed at something Flora McGowan said and refilled her glass. She'd settled so much in the past weeks, finding her rhythm and her backbone, blooming in a way he hadn't expected. However different it was from where she'd started, she fit here. But wouldn't staying limit her world in a wholly different way? Much as he couldn't imagine life without her now, he didn't want that for her. He wanted her to have the freedom to soar in whatever way she wanted.

Was there some kind of middle ground where they had a chance at anything other than a brief affair?

"You look like you're having deep thoughts."

Ewan blinked at George Davidson, who'd sidled up to the bar. "Suppose I am. What can I getcha?"

"Oh, I'm here for business, not pleasure. I came to pick up the information packet to be sent out to all the bands."

"The what for the what?"

"The Battle of the Bands the pub is hosting this weekend to decide who's playing for the Highland Games festival this year. They need information on when to arrive, where to set up, what equipment will be provided."

"What the hell are you on about? I'm not hosting a Battle of the Bands."

"Yes, you are." Ciara slid up beside him. "We signed the pub up to host while you were away on your holiday in the wilds."

"You did what?"

His sister just continued, as if all this was a foregone conclusion. "It's going to be great publicity and brilliant fun."

Temper began to kindle. "We canna host something like that."

"Why not? We've had live music before."

"Sure. Once in a while. One-off performances by the likes of The Kilt Lifters. No' something that's going to draw a real crowd." Crowds meant strangers. More factors he couldn't control. Potential threats to Isobel's safety.

"Oh, we thought of that," George put in. "Sold tickets so the pub wouldn't be over capacity. It's going to be a big event."

Ewan folded his arms. "We're no' doing it."

George gave him a pitying stare. "I'm afraid it's too late to cancel now."

"No one told me. We havenae ordered additional food and drink to cover the additional crowds."

"Yes, we did," Laura sang out as she carried an order from the kitchen.

He scowled after her. "Is every-fucking-body in on this but me?"

Ciara just grinned. "Mostly."

"You didnae have the right to make such a decision." The glare he shot her had cowed men twice her size.

She shrugged. "Too late now."

"She's right."

"And if I refuse?"

"Then the council can make life difficult for you," George said equably.

Ewan knew that to be true. He'd managed to stay on the village council's good side since he'd bought the pub, but he knew other business owners in town who'd run afoul of the group. As the only pub in town, he didn't think they could do anything to put him out of business—the citizens of Glenlaig would riot—but they could give him a lot more headaches, and he didn't need that shite.

Running a frustrated hand through his hair, he tried one more time. "I dinna ken the first bloody thing about how to set up for an event like that. Where the hell would we even fit a stage?"

Isobel stepped up to the bar. "Back corner. The acoustics are best there, and it's ready access to the outdoor patio area, which is the obvious place to bring equipment in and out between performances. And if you shift the pool table into the private party room in the back, you'd easily be able to arrange the tables to accommodate for the flow of people." She whipped out her order pad and flipped a page over, drawing a quick map of the building and demonstrating in great detail exactly what she was talking about.

Ewan stared at her.

"See? Isobel has it handled," Ciara insisted.

It seemed she did. In so many ways, she'd come across as young and inexperienced, but this was clearly her world. A small version of it, at least. It was fascinating to see the confidence she had around an actual area of expertise.

He knew he was going to get overruled. This event was

happening with or without him—damn his staff. But he
wanted to make sure she was okay with it. "Are you sure?"

Her eyes sparked with an enthusiasm he hadn't seen before.
She patted his arm. "Leave it to me. I'll take care of it."

And with no further input from him, she turned to George.
"Tell me what you need."

## 11

By Saturday morning, the entire pub had been reorganized according to Isobel's exacting specifications. The pool table moved. Tables rearranged. Equipment set up. The flow checked and rechecked. The project had been a good distraction from Ewan, who, regrettably, hadn't kissed her again.

Oh, he hadn't rejected her. Hadn't pulled back. At home, he was cautiously affectionate. Who knew such a big, broody badass would be a cuddler? And she loved snuggling up with him on the couch, catching up on the list of shows Isla and the others insisted she had to watch. But that was as far as it had gone. Apparently, when he'd said "careful" he'd actually meant glacial. As that was definitely not what she'd had in mind, she'd appreciated having something else to think about besides whether she had the guts to try to seduce him. So far, the answer was no.

He was all growly and scowly over the Battle of the Bands. Aside from being annoyed at not being consulted, she knew he worried about the event from a security standpoint, because this was definitely bringing in a lot of people. A lot of strangers.

A lot of elements he couldn't control. She had her own concerns on that front, but this was a relatively local competition, with bands who largely wouldn't be known outside the region. Her review of the competitor list told her that much. She didn't know any of them personally, and that was as good as she could expect. There was still some worry that one of them might recognize her, but between the hair, the extra few pounds she'd finally put on—much to Dom's satisfaction—and subtle use of some makeup to alter her look even further, she thought she was safe.

So far, no one had paid her much mind, beyond following her instructions for loading and unloading equipment. She'd been running sound checks all morning, making note of settings for each group. The pub would open at eleven, as usual, so she'd arranged it such that the last sound check was the first band who'd be playing once patrons arrived. It felt so damned good to be at least adjacent to music again. She hadn't anticipated exactly how lost she'd feel without it.

Even though she didn't know any of the groups, these were her people. Fellow musicians. More, they were the sort of musicians her father had been. Bands who played mostly for the joy of it. For bragging rights or pints. None of them had been tainted by massive commercial success, and it did Isobel's soul good to be near them. To remember what it had been like in the beginning. Before she'd been paraded as a prodigy. Before her music had been hemmed in by the bottom line and expectations from Paul and her label.

The band currently on the makeshift stage was heavy on the Celtic undertones, their fiddle player front and center. A slim woman with curly red hair and a constellation of freckles across her cheeks, she bent and swayed like a reed in the wind, playing with her whole body. Her blistering licks made Isobel itch to join in, to add harmony, to be *part* of something again.

At this point, it had been nearly a month since she'd so

much as held a violin, let alone played one, so when the band finished their number, she eyed that fiddle like an addict jonesing for a fix. The yearning was deep and visceral, and evidently it showed.

"Do you play?"

Isobel blinked at the fiddle player—Soairse, she remembered—taking in her easy smile and the faint gleam of sweat at her temple from the exertion of her performance. "I used to."

The words gave her a pang. When she'd made the choice to run, leaving her violin had been a matter of survival. A chance to buy her more time and confuse the issue of whether she'd left of her own volition. She'd known she couldn't pursue work related to music. That would've made it too easy for Paul to find her. But she hadn't fully appreciated what she'd been giving up. She hadn't thought far enough ahead to consider whether she had to give it up for good. It wasn't the performance she missed. It was the outlet music gave her. She needed the release.

"Do you want to have a go?"

*More than anything in the world.*

But was it safe? Isobel glanced around the pub. They wouldn't open the doors to the ticketed crowd for another half hour. Many of the other bands had dispersed until their allotted time slot. It was only a few musicians and the pub staff, most of whom were tied up with pre-service preparations. No one was paying attention to her. Ewan wasn't back yet from picking up extra supplies.

What would it hurt?

"If you really don't mind."

Soairse offered the instrument. Isobel switched off all the PA equipment. No need to mic any of this. Then she moved out from behind the soundboard and accepted the violin with reverence.

It wasn't hers. She didn't feel that sense of recognition and warmth. But the weight of it, the shape of it, felt right in her hands. Lifting it to her shoulder, she rested her chin on the edge and sighed with pleasure. Soairse handed her the bow, and something inside her clicked back into place. A missing piece returned home.

For long moments, Isobel simply held the instrument, with no particular notion of what to play. Not one of her pieces. That was too risky. And it wasn't classical or covers she was in the mood for. It was pure emotional expression of all the music that had been building inside her, dying to get out. Because, God, she needed that in the same way she needed a good orgasm. As *that* didn't seem to be on the horizon, she'd take what she could get.

Setting the bow to strings, she began to play.

At the first note, everything she'd held in, held back, began to pour out like some kind of geyser, until she wasn't the one in control anymore. She was simply a tool of the music, a vessel overflowing.

Closing her eyes, she let herself go.

EWAN'S NERVES WERE FRAZZLED. Despite the fact that Laura and Dom had adjusted their orders with assorted suppliers, he wasn't at all sure that they wouldn't run out of food or drink. Because the tickets had sold out. That didn't mean everyone would stay for the entire battle—that would be going on into the night—but he'd been on the phone half the morning with various locals, inquiring about last-minute replenishment of supplies, just in case. Then he'd had to go pick some up himself, leaving Isobel running sound checks.

With half an ear, he'd listened to her chatting and laughing with each group in a way he hadn't seen her do before. It was, he supposed, because they spoke a shared language. There was a wide array of quality among the competitors—from ear-split-tingly awful to actually enjoyable. From what he'd been told, each band would get twenty minutes for a set. At the end of the night, the ticket holders would vote. The top three groups would be invited back as headline entertainment during the upcoming Highland Games.

It wasn't the worst idea ever. And if he didn't have Isobel's safety to worry about, he likely would have agreed. Eventually. After some arguing.

Okay, so he would've said no on principle because he didn't like people this much. Having so many strangers in his space left him edgy. There were too many variables to keep up with, and it pinged his personal radar as too many threats, not enough intel.

The village was overrun with people. Not as it would be during the games themselves, but far more than normal. He scowled, fingers drumming the steering wheel as he fought traffic to get back to the alley to offload the local pork, bushels of potatoes and carrots, and the additional keg of locally brewed beer. They'd be opening soon, so all this needed to be prepped and put away.

Dom and Archie met him at the door.

"Gonna be a wild one," Dom predicted. "These extra supplies will come in handy."

"I trust you'll be able to figure out something to do with it."

"Have I ever failed you?"

"You have not. Are they finished with soundchecks?"

"I think so. Or nearly."

They hauled everything inside. Ewan left Dom to deal with the pork while he wrestled the keg into the cooler.

When the first note sounded, he knew. Even before he turned, he *knew* it was Isobel. He didn't understand how, but he could hear her in the music. She stood alone on the little stage, eyes closed, a violin in her hands, as she played something from the depths of her soul.

It wasn't a song he recognized. He wasn't even sure this was some formally composed thing. But he could hear her story. She began with grief. Each lonely note reached into his chest and squeezed as she painted a picture of isolation and longing. Fear rose up beneath it. The undertone of it bled into a frantic rhythm that mimicked her panicked escape and the wildness of the storm. It sent him back there, to the wind and rain on that empty stretch of road. The minor key shifted to something brighter, bolder, and he recognized himself in the melody, felt her relief at salvation. The transition was soft and slow, mirroring the safe place and comfort he'd given her. With each note, he heard the blooming he'd watched over the past weeks.

And he could see it as she stood, wringing every possible drop of emotion from an instrument that seemed to be an extension of her. Gone was the uncertainty. Gone was the fear. Gone was everything young and inexperienced and incapable. In its place was a completely self-contained, self-composed professional.

Ewan was utterly captivated. This was who she really was, and it was awe-inspiring. That confidence, that magic at her fingertips, was sexy as hell. Her face was full of so much wonder and feeling. Passion. He couldn't help but wonder if this was how she'd look when she came apart.

When the last notes died away, she sighed, her whole body relaxing in a way she hadn't the entire time he'd known her. Then she opened her eyes and looked straight into his. Her look was intimate and devastating, and his answering punch of lust was instant.

Christ, he needed this woman.

Stunned silence reigned for several beats. Then someone started clapping. Then everyone was clapping.

Ewan barely heard, cutting through the tables and lingering musicians with the sole goal of getting to her.

Isobel blinked, seeming to come out of a trance. Color

streaked her cheeks as she handed the instrument back to its owner, who shook her head with a grin.

"Well, fuck. That was amazing. What the hell are the rest of us doing here?"

He caught her by the hand.

The eyes she turned up to him were a little bit wary. "You're back."

"I am. Excuse us."

Without another word, he towed her down the hall, into the office. Now was the time to say something about knowing who she was, about doing whatever was necessary to free her, so she didn't have to hide this. Hide who she was.

But the moment they were inside and he'd shut the door, he found himself backing her against it. He knew he was crowding her with his body, caging her in, violating his own rules. Her hands slid up his chest, but she didn't push him away. "Isobel—"

Her throat worked. "I know I shouldn't have drawn attention—"

"I dinna care. You were pure dead brilliant." He wondered if she'd play him as skillfully as she'd played that fiddle. "You played... us."

Pleasure lit her eyes. "Yes."

"That was basically the hottest thing I've ever seen. You're amazing."

"You've given me a lot to work with." Her fingers curled into his shirt and pulled him closer, chest to chest, hip to hip.

That was all it took for the last of his resolve to crumble.

His mouth crashed down on hers, desperate to taste her again. He tried to slow down, to find some gentleness, but Isobel opened for him, and at the first brush of her tongue against his, he went a little mad. All his restraint, all his good intentions evaporated, his fingers digging into her hips, hauling her tighter against his erection. With a little whimper, she slid her hands higher, over his shoulders, and pulled. Absolutely on the same page, he gripped her legs and lifted so she could wrap them around his waist, and oh dear God, yes. He found himself wishing he'd worn his kilt and that she'd put on that little sundress so they could find some sweet relief. Instead, his cock pressed hard enough against his fly, he was certain the zipper would be permanently imprinted. He pivoted to the desk, wondering if he could get her jeans down her legs—and promptly knocked into a chair.

Stumbling, he barely kept from dropping her as he twisted so it was his arse that hit the desk hard enough to rattle it.

For a long moment, they stared at each other, breathing hard.

Isobel began to giggle, quietly at first, then hard enough to shake against him.

As that just gave his dick unnecessary encouragement, he took a firmer grip on her backside, so she couldn't wriggle against him. "For the love of all that's holy, dinna move, woman."

She stilled, pressing her lips together in some semblance of a sober expression.

Because that doe-eyed innocence just made him want to kiss her again, he pressed his brow to hers and worked on getting himself under control. "Sorry."

"For what, exactly?"

*For nearly taking you like an animal against a door.* Yeah, no. He didn't much want to say that out loud. They were in his workplace, for fuck's sake.

"This wasnae what I brought you in here for."

"Why did you bring me in here?"

"I wanted to—"

The office door swung open. "Sweetheart, we wanted to let you know we're—Oh!"

In complete shock, Ewan watched his mother—*his mother*

—stop dead in her tracks at the sight of him leaning against his desk, with Isobel's legs wrapped intimately around him.

"What is it, Bonnie?" Before Ewan could do anything to rectify the horror of the situation, his father joined her in the doorway. "Oh! Sorry, son. We'll just give you a minute. Or five." Grabbing Bonnie by the elbow, James tugged her back and shut the door.

"Son?" Isobel squeaked. "Those were *your parents?*"

"Aye. I'm afraid so."

"And they just saw us like...*this?*"

"It seems so."

"Put me down!"

He straightened, and she unwound her legs, stumbling back the moment she touched the floor.

"Oh, my God. Oh, my God!" Her cheeks flamed with embarrassment. "Please tell me there's a secret exit from this room because I cannot go out there after that."

"Sadly, no. Besides which, they ken where I live, so they'd just show up there next."

She squeezed her eyes shut. "I could have gone my entire life without this particular level of mortification."

"I'm no' particularly keen on it myself."

Squaring her shoulders, she straightened her shirt and combed both hands through her hair. "Okay, how do I look?"

There was no hiding those well-kissed red lips or the lingering look of arousal in her eyes. "Um. Like you've been properly snogged against a door."

Wilting into the chair, she groaned. "That's it then. I live here now. I can never leave."

"And I can?" He looked pointedly at the erection that still hadn't died, despite the interruption.

"First your dog. Now your parents. I'm starting to think this is a sign."

Ewan caught her hand. "It's not. It's just a reminder that we need to think about important things. Like locks. And privacy."

Her gaze snapped back to his. "So you're... not backing off?"

"I think it's obvious I'm not. Not unless you want me to."

Her fingers tightened around his. "I don't."

"Okay. We do have to actually get back out there. The doors open soon, and there's work."

Wincing, she glanced at the door. "Do you think they might've left?"

"I doubt it. The only way out is through." He tugged her to her feet. "C'mon. You've faced scarier things than this."

"I'm not sure I have," she muttered. But she let him pull her to the door.

After adjusting himself, he took a breath and stepped outside.

His parents hadn't gone far. They stood at the end of the hall, conversing with Ciara.

"Mum. I didnae think you'd be back for another couple of days. Is everything alright?"

She beamed and wrapped her arms around him, topping out somewhere around his chin. "Everything is just fine. The trip was lovely, but they were having a horrible heat wave in Greece, so we decided to come back a little early. And Ciara tells us there's a lot going on here." Her gaze slid back to Isobel, and she grinned. "I can see she's right. Hello, dear. I'm Bonnie McBride, and this is my husband James. It's so lovely to meet you."

With a glare for his sister, who was grinning like the cat who ate the canary, Ewan put an arm around Isobel and pulled her into his side. If his entire staff wasn't aware of what had been going on in that office, no doubt they would be within the next ten minutes. "Mum, Da, this is Isobel Donnchadh." He deliberately didn't label her. They hadn't had that discussion, and he didn't want to give any more fuel to the gossips.

"Hello."

James extended his hand and folded Isobel's into it for a shake. "Delighted." Over her head, he winked. "Well done, son."

"Da!" The warning tone that had made multiple enemy combatants back down had zero effect on his father. James just grinned.

"Of course, you'll both come to Sunday lunch tomorrow," Bonnie insisted. "We want to hear all about you! Ciara's been dreadfully sparse on the details."

"I was sworn to secrecy," Ciara declared.

"Clearly not thoroughly enough," Ewan muttered.

His sister just blew him a kiss. "Lunch should be perfect, mum. Himself here is actually closing the pub to give us all a day off since today it's all hands on deck. Isnae that nice of him?"

He was already regretting that decision. But before he could come up with some other excuse, Isobel straightened with resolve. "Thank you for the invitation. What can we bring?"

## 12

Isobel went with flowers. Flowers were always appropriate, right? Plus, Sophie had assured her that dahlias were Bonnie's favorite. Isobel figured she needed all the help she could get to overcome the eyeful his parents had walked in on. An eyeful that hadn't even gotten followed up on last night because the Battle of the Bands had run late. And after a sixteen-hour day, she'd fallen asleep in the Land Rover on the way home. Hard enough that Ewan had carried her inside to bed. Hers. The warm bulk she'd woken to this morning had been Havoc. And while she adored the dog, he definitely hadn't been her preferred bedmate.

She might've thought Ewan was retreating again, but for the fact that he clasped her hand in his on the drive. Given the tension in his frame, she thought he might be more nervous than she was.

"Are you okay?"

"Fine." The single syllable was short, clipped.

"Aye, you sound it."

Ewan sighed. "Sorry. It's just... I've never done this before."

"Done what?"

"Brought a woman home to my parents."

The words echoed in her head, implying a seriousness, a permanence that she didn't know what to do with. "Is that what this is?"

"That's certainly what they'll think this is."

"Ah. Right." Isobel ignored the disappointment that coursed through her. Of course he wasn't looking at something serious. It had been a month. He didn't even know who she was. At least, not the whole of her.

"That disnae mean it's not what it would have been. Eventually. If we'd been left to sort things out on our own time. Mum's just likely to want to move up the timeline."

"There's a timeline?"

"In her mind, there is. She wants to see me settled. Wants grandchildren."

"Oh." *Children?* Isobel definitely didn't know what to say to that. She'd never considered whether she wanted them one way or the other. That had always seemed premature when she'd barely even dated. "I... um..."

"It's getting miles ahead of things. We're still figuring this thing out between us. Add to that your unique situation, and I'm bracing to run interference."

"I'm sorry I've brought so much more stress into your life."

He whipped the 4x4 onto a dirt road and threw it into park, turning toward her across the center console. "You've brought a lot of things into my life. Stress isn't one of them. I dinna have regrets about stopping in that storm."

Her heart leapt at the intensity in his gaze. "Neither do I."

They stared at each other, longing pulsing between them.

"I'd kiss you, but we've established I'm no' so good at stopping, and I dinna think you want me to muss you up before we get to lunch."

She laughed a little. "If you knew how much time I've spent thinking about you mussing me up, you might not say that. But no, I'd like to at least attempt to behave with proper decorum in front of your parents."

He blew out a breath and put the vehicle back into gear. As he eased into motion again, she couldn't quite stop herself from provoking him. "But you did arrange for a full day off, so I feel compelled to say that I wouldn't be opposed to mussing later on."

The eyes he turned on her were hot. "Well now, that's just mean. How am I supposed to think about anything else for the next couple of hours?"

Isobel patted his leg. "You've shown heroic restraint for most of a month. I think you'll manage."

"And here I thought you were innocent." His smirk said he was teasing.

"Only mostly." She'd had exactly one lover, and while he'd been sweet, the experience had been underwhelming. Isobel couldn't imagine anything about Ewan being underwhelming. Her mind helpfully reminded her how it had felt to be pinned against the door by his bulk, her legs wrapped around his hips, and heat swept through her.

Well, damn it, now she wouldn't be able to think about anything else for the next couple of hours, either.

*Brought it on yourself, girl.*

She turned her mind to music, mentally playing through a couple of Mozart concertos to get herself under control.

Ten minutes later, they arrived at the single-story white bungalow where Ewan told her he'd grown up. Bonnie had opened the door and come out before they'd even unfastened their safety belts.

*Show time.*

Isobel slid out of the car, and as Ewan was cornered for hugs, she retrieved the flowers from the backseat.

Beaming, Bonnie turned from her son and reached out. "Welcome! We don't stand on formality here, and I'm a hugger."

With a quick, panicked look at Ewan that did nothing but make him pluck the flowers from her hands so they wouldn't be crushed, Isobel found herself folded in. Bonnie felt like a mom. Isobel didn't know any other way to describe the soft, warm embrace. The inherent comfort of it had tears stinging her eyes. She'd been hugged so little since her mother died. Quick, friendly squeezes. The occasional affection from a date. But not this all-encompassing sense of... acceptance. She found herself squeezing back, wanting to soak up the sensation.

Some of the nerves had settled by the time Bonnie released her. They simply slid away in the face of her unmistakable warmth.

"There now. Come in. Lunch is nearly ready. Ciara's already here."

"I... um... got you flowers?" Isobel cursed herself for making it sound like a question.

Ewan handed them over. "Sophie sends her best."

"Oh, that Sophie. Always kens my favorite." Bonnie buried her face in the blooms. "Just lovely. Thank you both. I'll get these in water."

The house was warm and cozy. It looked lived in, with scuffs on the wood floors and dings in the woodwork. In one doorway, she spotted lines and dates, with Ciara and Ewan's initials carved into the wood. A height chart, Isobel realized with delight. She loved that. Loved the idea that it was a home where people actually lived, where they built a history, not some showpiece. Photos of the family were everywhere, and she eagerly drank in the sight of a younger Ewan in rugby kit, arm around his father. He'd been tall even then, but not as broad, certainly not as gruff. There were others of a teenaged Ewan playing pony for a very young Ciara, who wore fairy wings and a crown. It was more than evident they adored each other. He was less obvious in his affections now, but she'd observed enough the past month to know that his sister still largely had him wrapped around her finger.

The dahlias made a lovely centerpiece on the big farm-house table. They ate family style, serving themselves from the dishes and bowls clustered in the center. Conversation flew fast and furious around her, and Isobel soaked it up, curious about these people who'd raised the kind, brave, honorable man who'd taken her in, given her place. Stolen her heart. And as she watched the teasing and the talking, saw the obvious joy they all took in each other, she fell a bit in love with his family, too.

"How long have you lived here?"

James tore into his dinner roll and considered. "Oh, thirty-five years this spring."

Bonnie picked up the thread. "We bought it expecting to just have the one child. And then we got surprised with Ciara when he was ten, so we added on to get some more space. Do you have any siblings, Isobel?"

"No. I was an only child. That must've been quite the challenge, having two with such a big age gap."

James laughed. "We weren't thrilled to be dealing with nappies again, that's for certain. But she was such a dear, we got over it."

Ciara batted long lashes at her father. "It's because I am an utter delight."

"And so shy about it, too," Ewan muttered dryly.

"You love me."

"I canna imagine why."

Isobel kept asking questions, satisfying her curiosity and keeping the focus off herself. She'd gotten good at that over the past month. But eventually, his mother wouldn't be distracted.

"Now, Isobel, tell me all about you."

Beside her, Ewan tensed.

She caught his eye, shook her head. This was a safe space.

She understood that. So she'd give them a little. "That's... complicated. I escaped an abusive situation and got into a wreck in the middle of nowhere in the middle of the night in the middle of a storm. Your son is the one who rescued me. And he's been kind enough to let me hide out here ever since, giving me a job and a place to stay."

Given the shock on their faces, obviously Ciara hadn't divulged that part when reporting about the goings on at home.

Bonnie's hand reached out to cover hers on the table. "I'm so sorry, my dear. If there's anything we can do to help, we certainly will."

"I appreciate that."

James opened his mouth, probably to ask more questions, but Ewan intervened. "We willnae be discussing it." The finality in his tone shut everyone up.

His father nodded, accepting the declaration with equanimity. "Right. So you play violin?"

"Not that any of us knew that before yesterday," Ciara grinned. "Sneaky minx."

Still a tricky subject, but Isobel could talk about this a little. She forked up a bite of roasted potatoes. "Aye, my father taught me when I was young."

"He taught you very well. That performance was amazing."

"Seriously awe-inspiring," Bonnie added.

"Oh, I didn't realize that you were there." Then again, she hadn't been aware of anybody the whole time she'd been playing.

"We weren't, but we saw the video."

As James' words sank in, the blood drained from Isobel's face so fast, her head spun. "What video?"

"Oh, you totally went viral." Ciara pulled out her phone and opened something before passing it over.

Isobel took it with a trembling hand and stared at the clip of herself. "No, no, no, no."

"Did you film this?" Ewan demanded.

"No, of course not. One of the other musicians did, I think."

Ten minutes. She'd played for ten full minutes. And someone had filmed the whole thing.

The video had racked up more than a million views since yesterday, and that was just on this site. She knew how social media worked. Knew there was no putting the genie back in the bottle.

This was the reason she'd cut herself off from music. Because this was exactly what she'd been afraid of. It had been a risk. A gamble. And she'd lost.

"I shouldn't have played. I shouldn't have touched it. I knew better. And now this is out there... everywhere. He's going to find me."

She'd ruined everything. She'd have to run. Again. Where would she go? What would she do?

Panic gripped her like a fist, constricting her chest, her throat. She heard her breath wheezing, felt her body quaking. She heard a low curse, then her chair was yanked back, and Ewan hauled her straight into his lap, wrapping around her.

"Breathe. Isobel, look at me."

She lifted her head.

Ewan held her tight, his expression utterly calm. "Breathe."

She did as he ordered. One breath. Two. More. With every inhale, the scent of him surrounded her. And the panic began to ebb.

He gripped her nape, kneading softly. "He willnae get near you. It's gonna be okay."

She wanted to believe him. Wanted to think he could conquer anything that tried to hurt her. "How?"

"Do you trust me?"

Isobel nodded once. Of course she trusted this man. He'd become her safe harbor. Her shelter.

"We bring in Hamish to finally deal with this, once and for all. Stop running and address it head-on."

The idea of it paralyzed her. But so did the prospect of walking away from what she'd found here.

Ewan just waited, patient and steady. "You're no' alone anymore."

He'd fight for her. He'd put himself between her and anything or anyone who meant her harm. She understood that. She treasured that.

If she wanted to keep this life, she had to find the courage to fight for it.

So she nodded. "Okay."

HAMISH MIGHT HAVE BEEN DRESSED for painting in ratty jeans and an old t-shirt, but he was every inch the lawyer as he invited them inside the farmhouse he and his daughter now called home. Isobel remembered from the dinner at Lochmara that the house was over two-hundred years old and had been added onto time and time again. It showed in the warren of rooms, many of which bore signs of recent repairs or paint, as he led them through to the kitchen.

Freya looked up from where she'd been painting trim on the glassed-in sunroom off the back. A streak of white trailed down one cheek. "Hi, Ewan. Isobel."

Too wound up to speak, Isobel just waved.

Beside her, Ewan uttered a tight, "Hey," of acknowledgement. Since they'd left his parents' house, he'd been in what she thought of as mission mode—focused, aware of everything and everyone, ready to act at a moment's notice. She knew Paul wouldn't come at them like the enemy combatants Ewan had faced down during his military service, but his confidence and competence helped steady her for what was to come.

Registering the seriousness of their visit, Hamish addressed his daughter. "Freya, love, why don't you take a break? We've got some boring grown-up things to talk about."

"Hooray!" She leapt up and started for the door.

"Aren't you forgetting something?"

The girl did an about-face, bringing her paintbrush to the counter and wrapping it in plastic wrap before sticking it into the freezer. Then she popped the top back onto the can of paint. "Now can I go?"

"Go—" The door was already slapping behind her before he got out the rest of it. "—ahead."

Shaking his head with amusement, Hamish turned back to them both. "I'll put the kettle on, if you want to have a seat."

Ewan pulled out a chair for Isobel, then took the one next to her, close enough his leg brushed hers. She twined her fingers with his and leaned into him, absorbing his ready strength. He brushed a kiss to her temple and held on.

God, she hoped he kept hanging on, even once he had the full truth.

A few minutes later, Hamish brought three mugs to the table and sat across from them. "Now, how can I help?"

After so many weeks of prevarication and hiding, the prospect of telling her truth was both terrifying and liberating. No sense in putting it off, though. Her happy little bubble had burst, and the only way out was through. She took a deep, shuddering breath and blew it out. "Isobel Donnchadh was the name I was born with. But because it's hard to spell, and people didn't know how to pronounce it, it was legally changed. The name the rest of the world knows me by is Elizabeth Duncan."

The mug in Hamish's hand thumped against the table, and his jaw went slack. "Oh!"

And there it was. The recognition she'd been half-expecting since she'd arrived in Glenlaig. "I take it you've heard of me?"

"Who hasn't? My wife and I—ex-wife—heard you in

London a few years back. You're one of my favorite musicians. It is an honor to meet you."

Under other circumstances, she'd have been flattered and a little embarrassed. But now she was too worried about Ewan. She searched his face, looking for traces of anger or condemnation or... something. But his expression hadn't changed at this new information. Because... it wasn't new.

"You're not surprised."

"No."

"Did you know who I was?"

"No' like that. I checked your ID that first night. I didnae want to invade your privacy, but I needed some notion of what I was protecting you from. Who you were."

Could she fault him for that? She'd been a stranger in trouble, who could've brought God knew what to his doorstep. "So you looked into me?"

"Indirectly. One of my former mates from the military is good at that sort of thing. I had him do some looking, so I'd ken who might be searching for you. What was out there."

"So... all this time you knew?"

"Not everything. He put together a dossier going back to the beginning."

"A dossier?" she echoed. This wasn't just doing some internet searches. This was... more. A hell of a lot more.

All this time, she'd been so grateful he hadn't pushed her. So relieved at his apparently boundless understanding and patience. And all along, he'd known everything. Or whatever his friend with skills could dig up.

She pulled her hand free, needing some space between them.

"I didnae read all of it. I just focused on the immediate threat. I wanted to give you the chance to tell me yourself. It wasnae about not trusting you. I was about being able to protect you in the best possible way."

It made sense from his perspective. She knew him well enough to understand that this was how he was wired, how he'd been trained to approach a threat. And she could admit to herself that, if he'd asked outright—and he had—she'd have balked on telling him the truth sooner.

"I didn't make that easy on you." Lifting the mug, she rolled it between her palms, absorbing the warmth and wishing she felt it deeper than her hands.

"You had no reason to trust me in the beginning. I've never held that against you."

He'd given her every reason to trust him since. Was she really going to hold this against him?

Hamish cleared his throat, reminding them both he was there. "If I may suggest that you start at the beginning?"

Right. They were here for a reason.

"I suppose for this to make sense, I have to go way, way back." Isobel sipped at her tea for fortification, then set the mug back down. "I could play violin almost before I could walk. My father—he was a music teacher—encouraged that gift. When I'd outstripped what he could teach me, he moved us around to find others I could learn from. I ended up enrolled at the Royal Academy of Music when I was eleven."

"Holy shite." Judging by the shock in Ewan's voice, he had some concept of what a big deal that had been.

Still, Isobel shrugged. "I only attended for a semester. Not because I couldn't hack the theory and the work, but because my father died. And without his income as a teacher, my mother couldn't make enough on her own to cover our living expenses. So I started performing. She didn't push me into it. It was my idea. I knew I was good. I'd done some performances at the school, and I got a lot of attention. People liked to bandy about the term 'prodigy,' and I guess maybe I was, being the caliber of musician I was at that age. Anyway, that's when we met Paul."

"Paul?" Hamish prompted.

"Paul Burgette. He's my manager and agent. He got me the gigs, then the recording contracts. In a very real way, he launched my career. And because he did, we had enough to keep a roof over our heads and food in our bellies. More than, for the first time in our lives. And, for a while, it was great. I got to perform. I got to share the thing that I loved with everyone. I was touring nationally at twelve. Internationally, by the time I was thirteen. Mum and I were happy. So, when Paul offered an exclusive contract for representation and management, she signed for me, since I was a minor and couldn't do it myself. I didn't see the contract. I didn't know the details, and Mum trusted Paul. He'd already treated us well. Gone out of his way. Done all of these things to take care of us. So she didn't have it reviewed by her own lawyer. She just signed it."

Hamish uttered a short, succinct, "Fuck. Go on."

Because everything went downhill from here, she sipped at the tea again. "My mother died when I was fifteen. Killed by a hit-and-run driver in Rome. I was devastated. At some point, she'd updated her will to name Paul as my guardian. And that was fine. He'd been the adult in my life for years by then. A father figure, though he could never replace mine. He took care of me. Took care of all the details I was too young or over-whelmed to manage myself. That's what Paul does. Handle the details, so I never had to worry about anything but the music. It was so easy to let him because staying in the music was easier than facing the grief. And that's how I process the world."

"That's what you were doing yesterday, when you played," Ewan murmured.

That he had not only heard himself—heard them—in the music, but recognized this said so much she wasn't quite ready to think about yet. It told her he understood her in a way no one had since her father. That had to factor into all of this. But not yet. There was still more story to tell.

She nodded, sipped at the tea again, though it had gone lukewarm. "After I turned eighteen, I started getting itchy, wanting something different. Starting to want to stretch my wings. I didn't have anything resembling a normal childhood. I'd had tutors, an education, but no school. I started to crave that. I wanted to go to university, like everyone else. But when I made noises about it, he kept reminding me that I'm not like everyone else. And how I had all these people who depended on me for a living. That kept me where I was, doing what I was doing. He learned that was a really great way of keeping me in line, and he was generally subtle about it. He's good at manipulation and control, and I was over twenty-one by the time I started to recognize that he'd effectively cut me off from making connections with other people. We were never anywhere long enough for me to make real friends. Even the people we toured with, he made certain they kept their distance so that all I had was him."

It had been a lonely life, one brought into stark relief compared to the past weeks here with Ewan. She'd made those friends, begun forming those connections. And she didn't want to lose any of it.

"I was twenty-two the first time he laid hands on me. I'd been talking to this guy I was quietly dating. Another musician on the tour. We kept our relationship quiet because I didn't know what Paul would say or do if he found out. Elliot was the one who suggested I talk to somebody. Maybe think about looking for new representation. I had an appointment with another agent—and when I got ready to go to it, Paul intercepted me, passing on the news that Elliot had been in an accident. Had his hand crushed in a car door, and wasn't that a shame?" Tears filled her eyes. "He didn't say it outright, but it was obvious that he'd had it done. Somehow. Because of me. Because I dared to try to defy him."

Tears spilled over at the memory. "I was furious. Horrified.

Elliot was a brilliant cellist, and he lost everything because he'd tried to help me. So I reported the whole thing to the police. But they didn't believe me. I had no proof. And by the time they'd finished speaking to Paul, I came across as nothing more than a flighty, hysterical woman looking to stir up drama for my own amusement."

Ewan muttered a string of vicious curses. "That's no' how it's supposed to work."

"Maybe not. But it's how it did work. And when he got back to the hotel, he cornered me and let the mask drop for the first time. Let me see the anger underneath. He jerked me around a little—just enough to make his point, not enough to bruise. And he told me that if I ever defied him again, someone else would be the one to pay the price because he owned me. I scoffed at that. Told him he'd have nothing without me. I threatened to quit. To walk away from all of it."

He'd smiled then. A chilling, vicious curve of lips she'd never forget. "He calmly explained that the contracts my mother signed gave him ownership of all of my performances, all of my music. And that sure, I could stop, but I'd never see another pound, and I wouldn't be able to create anything new without it belonging to him." She looked down at her hands. "I'd already lost both my parents. Music was the only thing I still had, so I stayed. And I stopped fighting."

It shamed her to admit it. But she hadn't felt as if she had a choice.

"Yet you still ultimately left," Hamish prompted. "How did that come about?"

She told the rest of it, trying to keep the delivery short and to the point. But she cried in earnest by the time she got to the part about leaving behind her father's violin, unable to hold back the tide of grief. Ewan's hand closed over hers, lending strength, and Isobel held on, finishing out the story.

"So, I've been here hiding for the past month. I have no idea what press is out there. I don't know what he told anyone that night I didn't show for my performance, or what he said to the other venues on the tour. There are dates booked out through the end of the summer."

When Ewan tucked her closer, she didn't fight it. "I ken the answer to this. He contacted the police in the beginning, but since you're an adult and they could find no evidence of foul play, the investigation essentially stalled out. There's a story circulating that you broke your wrist, and the performances for the next couple of months have been cancelled."

Hamish tapped his fingers on the table. "What about the car?"

Isobel's eyes widened. "I hadn't even thought of that. We just left it there, under the tree. I paid in cash, and there was never the opportunity to get it registered before I ran, but still. Someone could make the connection."

"They won't. I called in some favors and made it disappear."

"You did?"

Ewan shrugged. "We're men with a certain set of skills. I didnae see any reason no' to use them."

Isobel was starting to understand that he hadn't been a mere soldier.

Before she could thank him again, he turned to Hamish. "So, what are her options?"

"I'm not an entertainment lawyer, but there are two separate issues here: his representation of you as your agent and the rights he has over your past work and performance proceeds. No matter what kind of contract you—or your mother—signed, there's nothing stopping you from firing him so that he can't represent you moving forward."

She stared at him. "Just like that? I can say no?"

"Just like that. He's had his hooks in you since you were young, so he's been in a position to brainwash or terrorize you into believing otherwise. But you definitely don't have to keep him on."

"Thank Christ," Ewan muttered. "What about the rest? Ownership of her work?"

"That I can't speak to without seeing the contract myself. The idea that you wouldn't see any income at all seems like overstatement, no matter how predatory the terms. You write your own music, correct?"

"I used to. And I still put together my own arrangements, but I haven't written new music in a couple of years. Paul didn't want me going off in new directions as a musician, either. Stick with what works. I haven't exactly been in the right headspace to compose, anyway, since the attack on Elliot."

"Okay. Well, as I suspect bad faith in this situation, the first thing I'd be inclined to do is request an audit of his books. If he's doing something underhanded there, he won't want to hand that over, so there will likely be a lot of hemming and hawing and stall tactics. Or to avoid it, he'll have to provide a copy of the signed agreement. If he doesn't supply either of those things, we take him to court to say we suspect there is no agreement."

The calm certainty in Hamish's tone should've been comforting. And yet...

"It's not that simple. Paul's not going to just let me go, no matter what's legal on paper. I'm his golden goose. His meal ticket. I'm the reason he has everything he has. He's not going to just let me walk away. And since I was foolish enough to play in public in a video that's gone viral, he's going to find me."

"Given he's not likely to take the news of losing you as a client particularly well—and I think we should draft a certified letter to that effect and send it immediately—it wouldn't be a bad idea for the two of you to get out of town. Lie low for a few days at least. I know that's something Ewan knows how to do. In the meantime, I'll start the necessary steps to untangle this mess."

"That would be amazing. But if we send a certified letter, isn't he going to know definitively where I am?"

"I still have connections to my old firm in Edinburgh. I can use their address for now. Do you have a pound?"

"I... what?"

"A pound."

She dug in her purse and came up with the coin. "Here."

Hamish closed his fist around it. "There. I'm officially your lawyer of record, and I can act on your behalf. Now, I suggest you both go pack."

"But what about when he shows up? Because it's not a question of if, it's when. He *will* come here. He'll see that video, and he'll know it's me."

Ewan shoved back from the table. "You leave that to me."

## 13

"If anyone shows up asking about Isobel or the woman in the video, put them off the scent. Send them on a wild goose chase somewhere else. Dinna give her name or any information about her or life in Glenlaig."

If Laura minded the afternoon summons on her day off or the dictatorial orders Ewan was snapping out, she didn't show it. She merely nodded. "I'll see that the word is spread."

He knew she would. The staff would have their backs, as would the lion's share of the locals. Isobel had won everyone over in the past weeks.

"You're my second in command, so you're in charge while we're gone. You've got my permission to do whatever needs doing to keep things running." Ewan hesitated. "I dinna ken how long that will be." He'd already been gone for two weeks, and orchestrating that had taken work.

"It'll take however long it takes. You do whatever's necessary to take care of our girl. We'll take care of the pub." And for Laura, it was as simple as that. Isobel was part of the pub family, and so was he.

In that moment, Ewan had to admit the truth. "It should've been yours."

"What?"

"The pub. It should've been yours."

Laura rolled her eyes. "Go on with ye. I couldn't afford to buy it, and Drummond's kids wanted to wash their hands of it. I'm where I'm supposed to be."

"I couldnae do this without you."

"'Course not. And dinna you forget it." Her cheeky grin faded. "How's Isobel?"

Ewan hadn't told Laura much. Only that there'd been a video of yesterday's performance that had gone viral, and out of an abundance of caution, they were leaving town in case her abuser caught wind of it and showed up looking. "Scared. Ciara's helping her pack."

"Poor lamb. She's come out of her shell so much the past month. Glenlaig's been good for her." She fixed him with a knowing look. "You've been good for her. She's been good for you, too. I dinna want to see either of you lose that sparkle you've got now."

He didn't know what to say to that. Things still felt a little rocky between them since his revelation about having had Conroy look into her. There'd been no opportunity to discuss it since they'd left Hamish. Ewan had been on the phone, giving orders and calling in favors, generally doing whatever was necessary to make this disappearing act happen for them both.

Laura patted his cheek. "I'll get out of your way. Give her my best, and safe travels."

"Thanks. I will."

Ewan stood on his front stoop, watching until her little hatchback disappeared at the end of his drive. Then he was moving again. He had a go-bag packed—long habit—and he knew how to travel light. But he took the time to load a few extra things into another bag. This was a different kind of mission, with different considerations. Fifteen minutes later, their stuff was loaded in the back of the Land Rover, and Havoc was howling his displeasure at being left behind.

Isobel looked almost as mournful as she crouched to wrap her arms around the dog. "Do we have to leave him?"

"If we have to run, that's much harder to do with a dog his size. It's safer for him here."

"I guess that makes sense." She rubbed her cheek against his fur. "I'll miss you, sweet boy."

"I swear, I'll take good care of him," Ciara promised.

"You ken where all his stuff is?" Ewan asked.

"I'll figure it out. Don't delay on my account." When Isobel straightened, Ciara took her hands. "I'm sorry for how things turned out."

"It's not your fault. And in the end, this is probably for the best. I promise I'll tell you everything when we come back."

Ciara pulled her in for a hug. "I'm holding you to that."

"We need to go."

His sister shot him a stern glare. "You bring her back safe."

"I will."

She insisted on hugging him, too. "I love you, big brother."

"Love you, too." Because he wanted to lighten the mood a bit, he tugged on the ends of her hair as he had when she was little. "Everything will be fine." He had to trust that was the truth. Hamish would handle the legal side, and he'd cover her physical safety.

With one last scruff of Havoc's ears, they got into the 4x4 and rolled out, leaving his sister behind. Isobel said nothing, only stared at the side mirror, watching the house disappear.

"It's just a temporary goodbye." Ewan hoped he wasn't lying.

She blew out a breath. "So, where are we going?"

"I've got a friend with a cabin that's off-grid. Perfect place to hide out for a while."

"The same friend who looked into me?"

"No. A different one."

She accepted that with a nod. "Okay."

Feeling miserable about the distance between them, he set out to explain himself again. "Listen, about the invasion of your privacy—"

"No. You did what you thought was best, and you did it with the best of intentions. You've done nothing but prove your trustworthiness from the moment we've met, so I don't have any right to be angry. You were right to do what you did. You needed to know, and I wouldn't have responded well to pushing. It was the right call. I just... wasn't expecting all that." She hesitated. "Would you have told me if this hadn't happened?"

"Eventually. I wanted it to be on your time. You've had enough pushing and manipulation. That was obvious even before I heard your story." He met her gaze across the center console. "I willnae ever push you, unless it's a matter of your safety." That was one promise he knew he could keep.

"Thank you."

He shook off her words. He'd had enough of her gratitude. That wasn't why he'd done any of this. If a deeper voice prompted him to analyze those reasons, he could ignore it. There were more pressing things to see to right now.

When he turned toward Ardinmuir, she straightened in her seat. "We're going to the castle?"

"Aye. We just have to pick something up first." Perhaps the stop was foolish. They needed to put miles between them and here. But he'd started making these arrangements yesterday, before all this had become necessary. If they were going to be holed up for a while, he thought this would make things easier on her.

Ewan's visions of a quick getaway died a swift death as he pulled around to the kitchen door and spotted multiple vehicles. Someone had been watching because the door opened as soon as he parked. Angus hustled out, a box in his hands.

Charlotte was right behind. "Pop the back. You can make room for this."

"What is all this?"

"Provisions, my boy," Angus informed him. "Biscuits for the road, fresh bread, and Charlotte brought soup and some casseroles to see you through a few meals until you get settled wherever you're going."

"There are sandwiches, too, for the road tonight," she added.

Ewan stared at them. "What? How?"

"Ciara called and told us you'd be headed out for a while until the rat bastard who's after Isobel can be sorted," Charlotte explained. "We can't go with you, so we're sending food."

Isobel's eyes went watery. "Oh, that's so lovely of you."

"Of course, sugar." She gave Isobel a motherly squeeze. "We've got your back."

Ewan's throat went a little thick as well. "How did you even ken we'd be stopping by?"

"That would be because of me." Munro stepped out of the house, a box in his hands as well. "I knew you wouldn't likely be leaving without this.

Ewan accepted the long, rectangular box. "Does that have everything we need?"

"It should do, aye."

"Thank you."

The older man's lips curved in an understanding smile. "You're more than welcome."

Connor and Sophie popped out.

Sophie immediately pulled Isobel into a hug. "Don't you worry. Kyla and I have everything covered to handle the fallout of the video."

"How?" Ewan demanded.

"Kyla's busy crafting a fake website under a fake name for our newly discovered musician. I'm putting together the social media to back it up. It won't stand up to anything really rigorous, but it's enough to confuse the issue and buy you some time."

"Smoke and mirrors," Connor added. "And just so you ken, I'll be taking on some shifts as bartender at the pub, so I can keep my ear to the ground, as it were."

Ewan had no idea whether any of this would actually work, but it couldn't hurt. Probably. Even if it just fucked with Burgette, it was worth it. "Let me give you the contact information for a friend of mine. He can help see that the site launches from an IP address far away from here. And thank you. All of you."

"Hey, after all the help you gave earlier this year, exacting some karma against—" At Sophie's side eye, Connor cut himself off. "—um... parties who shall remain nameless-if-not-blameless, we owe you."

Isobel looked between them with interest. "I feel like there's a story there."

Connor shot her a wink. "One, I could probably be induced to tell you over a pint or three when you get back."

Ewan couldn't quite hold in a snort. "You'd never last in covert ops, Cousin."

"And thank God, I dinna have to." He pulled Ewan in for a back-thumping hug. "Seriously, good luck and godspeed. We've got things handled here."

Staring at all these people who'd helped because they cared, Ewan believed it. That made it easier to let go of this piece so he could focus on what lay ahead.

They loaded the extra supplies and said final goodbyes, exchanging hugs and handshakes. Then Ewan put home in his rearview mirror and set a course to safety.

THE SUN WAS SETTING by the time the Land Rover rolled to a stop in the middle of nowhere. Isobel had lost track of where they were hours ago. She was pretty sure Ewan had done some kind of double- or triple-back to confuse a tail. Not that they'd had one, so far she knew. They'd left villages and even proper roads behind an hour ago, bumping along barely there tracks in the woods. She was positive she'd never been anywhere this remote.

"Are we camping here for the night?" He hadn't said anything about camping, but there was nothing else out here.

Ewan shut off the engine. "We're here."

"Here, where?"

"At the cabin."

Isobel looked around and saw nothing but rocks and trees. Certainly, there was no sign of habitation. "Where?"

"You'll see."

She followed him toward two massive boulders that made up part of the shoulder of the mountain. He shifted aside some debris to reveal a gap between the rocks. They created a little corridor that dog-legged out of sight. It was just wide enough for him to slip through. At his urging, she stepped inside, around the corner and... there was a door built right there into the rocks.

"Please tell me this is not actually a cave. Because I don't know if I can handle that."

"No." He slid aside a canny little panel on the rock to reveal a numeric keypad. With the punch of a few numbers, there was a click, and he opened the door. "Give me a minute to turn on the power."

Baffled, fascinated, she stood where she was until he called out for her to come inside after him. She stepped inside and lost her breath. Cabin wasn't precisely the right term, though there was ample wood and stone making up the structure. There was a flat space on the opposite side of the rocks, stretching maybe thirty feet by perhaps fifteen at the widest point. The structure had been built to hug the mountain, following its contours. Rock made up the walls on this side and even part of the floors. But the far wall was glassed in, showing breathtaking views of the setting sun and the valley beyond.

"Holy shite."

"Impressive, isn't it? The glass is non-reflective, so no one would see it from this side. Not that there's any easy way to access this side. With the door hidden from the other, no one would even ken it was here. It's entirely off-grid. There's solar for electricity and to heat the water, which is collected and stored in a cistern and filtered. There's a woodstove for heating and cooking. And that section there opens up to a wee balcony. There are folding chairs we can take out to sit, if you're okay with heights."

"Just... how? How would you even get work crews out here to build it?"

"He didnae have crews. He had us."

She turned wide eyes on him. "You helped build this place?"

"Aye. It technically belongs to Quinn, as he bankrolled the lot of it—family money—but it's been sort of a haven for all of us, as we've needed it."

Isobel wondered how often Ewan had been the one to need this place.

The whole space was one big room, save for a partition that likely marked the bathroom. It was simply furnished, with a rough-hewn table and chairs near the minimalist kitchen. A small sofa and coffee table faced that magnificent view. At the far end, a queen-sized bed with a simple green comforter was tucked against the wall. Or maybe built into it. Just the one bed. As there was no chance either of them could stretch out on the sofa, her heart began to thump in anticipation of the close quarters. But that was getting ahead of things. A lot had happened since that... interlude in the pub office—God, had that only been yesterday? Things still felt a little off between them after all the revelations, and she shouldn't make assumptions.

He headed for the door. "C'mon. Let's get our things."

They brought in the bags and all the food that had been pressed upon them. She began putting it away as Ewan went to stash the Land Rover... somewhere. She didn't ask. He was back ten minutes later, as she finished playing Tetris to fit all the containers in the small refrigerator.

"I'm pretty sure Charlotte made enough for at least a week."

"Charlotte shows her love through food. Angus, too."

And they'd made food for her. Well, not just her. Ewan, too. But she felt the affection and care that had gone into their efforts, and it warmed something inside. "Do you want me to pull something out for a late dinner?"

"I'm okay with the sandwiches and biscuits we had." He set one last box on the table.

"Is that more food? Because we've essentially filled the fridge and freezer. It's not that large."

"No." He rocked on the balls of his feet, an uncharacteristically nervous move. "But it is for you."

"For me?"

"Open it."

Curious, she opened the flaps and went still. A violin case nestled inside. Her eyes flew to his.

He just jerked a chin toward the box. "Keep going."

Gently, she lifted it from the box. The leather case was old and cracked, rough beneath her fingers. She flipped the latches to open it and lifted the lid. The instrument inside held the warm patina of age. She could feel the weight of years on it as she touched it with reverence. "Where did you get this?"

"I told you I'd run tame at Ardinmuir as a boy. It wasnae just outside. One of the things that goes along with an estate that old is that there's often a music room. They've got a multitude of instruments, and I remembered this was one of them. No one's played it in at least a few generations. After yesterday, I called Connor to ask if they'd mind loaning it out. Munro ran up to Inverness to pick up fresh strings and resin. I thought you'd had enough of being without the thing you loved and deserved a chance to indulge without fear. You can play here to your heart's content without anyone but me to hear you."

The wash of gratitude all but drowned her. That he would do this, think of this, to give her back the thing she'd had to leave for her own safety... There was no more precious gift. Nothing could have made her feel more seen and valued. More loved. And maybe that wasn't what this was for him. Maybe he was just that *good* of a man. But she loved him for it. Loved him for all of it.

And despite the fact that she could pick up that violin and play everything she was feeling, for once, something else had a greater pull. She wanted to show him.

Circling around the table, she stepped up to frame his stubbled cheeks and bring his mouth down to hers. He sighed into the kiss, settling his lips against hers, but he didn't take over, didn't push for more. He'd said in the car that he wouldn't push her for anything unless it involved her safety. If she wanted this, wanted him, she had to be the one who pushed.

Eyes half-closed, she murmured against his mouth. "Ewan, come to bed."

That rock-hard body went perfectly still against her. "Isobel, that's no' why—I dinna need—"

She nipped at his lower lip, then kissed away the sting. "I *do* need. I need you. I want you. Please."

His hand threaded through her hair, cupping her nape in that way he had that was at once possessive and soothing.

"We're going to be trapped here together for who kens how long."

She recognized the warning and deliberately pressed closer. "Good. Then there's no one to interrupt us this time."

If she'd thought his iron will might just snap, she was mistaken. He drew her in as he skated his hand down her spine to her cup her backside and pull her hips against his. The feel of his erection had her knees going loose and heat pooling low in her belly. He breathed her in, skimming his nose along her throat to her ear. "I want to devour you."

*Oh, God.*

Mouth dry, she let her head fall back in invitation. "No one's stopping you."

"But you can. At any point. Just say the word. I need you to ken that."

She wouldn't stop him, but his honor would demand she acknowledge that she could. "Okay."

He began to back her toward the bed. "Is there anywhere I cannae touch? Anything I cannae taste?"

Those husky questions had a feast of erotic images unfurling in her brain. "No."

"Good. Then I'm starting here." His fingers bunched the fabric of her blouse, skimming it up her torso and off. The reverent curse allayed any fear she might've had standing in front of him in her bra. He traced the edge of the cup, lighting little fires along the tops of her breasts before following the strap to the back and the clasp. A quick flick and she was free, her breasts spilling into his callused hands.

"Oh, God."

"You like that?"

"Your hands feel so good."

He cupped them around her, kneading her flesh, thumbing her nipples to needy peaks. "So lovely." When he circled one with his tongue, sucked it into his mouth, her knees buckled.

He caught her easily, holding her up so he could continue to suckle with a hum of pleasure. She speared her hands into his hair, holding him to her as he drowned her in sensation. Dimly, she registered the mattress at her back and wondered when he'd lowered them. Then she stopped wondering because his hands were at her belt, lowering the zipper of her jeans, and he was pressing kisses down the slope of her belly and lower, in that V of exposed skin.

Nerves kicked up as he pulled off her shoes and inched the jeans and knickers down, leaving her bare to his gaze in the last wash of sunset.

"Fucking gorgeous."

How could she feel anything but when his eyes roved over her with such hunger? So she didn't try to cover herself as he looked his fill.

When he lowered to his knees, her heart leapt into her throat. "Wait."

In an instant, his gaze was on hers. "No?"

"Maybe? I don't—I've never..."

"No one's ever done this for you?"

Isobel shook her head.

He sobered and sat back. "And the rest? Is this your first time?"

As she wasn't entirely sure he wouldn't stop if it was, she was grateful she didn't have to lie. "No. It's not. But I'm not exactly... um... experienced."

She wanted to squirm as he sat with that but made herself hold still.

At last, his lips curved in a wicked smile. "That just means I get to show you a whole new world. Good for me."

That smile promised every pleasure imaginable. And then some.

When she said nothing, Ewan pressed a tender kiss to the inside of one knee. "We can stop."

"No! Don't stop." Swallowing hard, she let her knees drop open. "Don't stop."

His eyes gleamed, and he curled those big hands around her calves, nudging them wider to make room for his shoulders. "I'll make you feel good. I promise."

Ewan McBride was nothing if not a keeper of promises. He made her feel better than good. He made her forget all the stress and strain and worry that had led them to this point. And in their place, he left her with unspeakable pleasure, taking her up, up, up with his mouth, his hands, until she splintered.

When she surfaced from the aftershocks, he was curled beside her, smirking with satisfaction. "Aye, I was right."

"About what?" she gasped.

"Just as sweet as I imagined."

Mustering some muscle control, she rolled into him, palming his erection through his jeans. "Not so sweet. Greedy. I want the rest of you." She needed him naked to level this playing field.

He nipped at her shoulder. "I needed you ready first."

"I'm more than ready now."

As he shed his clothes, and she got her first real look at the size of him, she nearly took it back. He was a big man... everywhere. "Um..."

Tossing the condom from his wallet to the bed, he stretched out beside her again. "Dinna worry. I willnae rush it. You'll be ready."

She had a few doubts, but they slipped away as he pulled her body against his and kissed her, long and deep. Under that coaxing play of lips and worshipful hands, her muscles unlocked, and she softened against him, glorying in the feel of skin against skin. It was an intimacy she hadn't known she craved, and now that she had it, she didn't want to let it go. Didn't want to let him go. So she was the one who wrapped around him, shoving him to his back, rolling on the condom, and straddling him until she could sink down, down, down.

He filled her up on every level—body, mind, heart. It wasn't the time to say it, so she took his mouth instead and began to move, pouring everything out with her body. He was her instrument, and as the whirl of emotion built inside her, she drove them both higher. His hands gripped her hips, matching her rhythm instead of restraining as he surged beneath her. And as they hit their crescendo and came apart together, she thought she'd never known sweeter music.

EWAN'S HEART thundered in his chest as Isobel wilted over him, limp with pleasure. Wrapping his arms around her, he nuzzled her brow, wanting nothing more than to burrow into this bed and stay here for the next decade or so. That might be enough time to sate himself. But practicalities needed to be dealt with. So he rolled them, ignoring how her body fluttered around his with aftershocks, already inspiring him to bury himself again before he'd even pulled out.

"Be right back."

She muttered a sleepy protest as he slipped away to deal with the condom. When he came back, she was curled on her side, her hair spread out against the pillow. But she wasn't asleep. Those prismatic eyes watched him as he climbed back into bed, her gaze skimming over him, tracing his tattoos and the lines of muscle, before dipping lower to his cock, which was already preening again at the attention.

"That was definitely not what happened after the last time I did this."

"It's no' exactly usual for me, either." He opened his arms, pleased when she snuggled close and tangled her legs with his. "It seems you stir my appetites. Which is a damned shame."

Isobel went still. "It is?"

"Aye. I only had the one condom in my wallet. We left in such a hurry, I didnae think about packing for this."

"Oh." She relaxed again. "That's okay. I did."

"You did?"

"I found the box in the bathroom and threw it in my bag. I thought it might come in handy."

The laugh bubbled up, vibrating his chest against hers. "Oh, you're just full of surprises."

"Good surprises?"

He rocked his hips against hers. "Definitely good surprises."

She wriggled a little, making his eyes cross as she pulled away.

"Are you okay? Did I hurt you?"

She pressed a kiss to his pec. "No. I'm just sensitive. It's been a while, and I definitely wasn't so thoroughly wrecked last time. I'm going to need a little time to recover."

He'd give her all the time she needed because he intended to wreck her again in a multitude of different ways if he got the chance. "How long is a while?"

"Two years."

Ewan did the math. "Was it the cellist?" He regretted the question as soon as it fell out of his mouth because she lost that languid relaxation.

"Aye. We were only together twice before the... Before." Her tone dripped with subdued grief.

Wanting to soothe, he stroked one hand down her graceful spine. "You canna blame yourself for what happened to him."

"Can't I?"

"No." Curling his fingers around her nape, he forced her gaze. "It's on Paul. He's the one who made it happen. He's the one at fault."

"That's true enough. But it doesn't change the fact that if Elliot had never met me, he'd still have a career. He'd still be able to play." She tucked her head back against his shoulder. "He's never spoken to me again."

"His loss." Ewan kissed her temple. "The bastard's going to be stopped. You're going to get out from under his hold." At her noncommittal murmur, he squeezed. "You *are*. Which begs the question—*when* you're free of him, what do you want?" He asked because he wanted her to think about it... and because he desperately wanted to know.

She sighed and began to trace little patterns on his chest. "I don't know. The idea of being free has always felt so out of reach. I never let myself dream beyond the concept."

That touch was driving him mad, waking up those over-sensitized nerve endings and inspiring a whole host of new fantasies to explore. But she needed time, and he'd asked the question. Struggling to keep his brain on the conversation, he reminded her, "You said you wanted normal. That was what made you fight in the first place."

"It was." She propped herself on his chest, peering down at him with so much emotion in her eyes. "You've given me a taste of that. You gave me a home. Family. Friends. All the things I've never had before. I couldn't hope to ever repay you for that gift."

"That's no' a thing you have to repay. It's a basic human right." And he'd give it all to her for the rest of his life if she let him. Because he realized she was it for him. She was the piece that had been missing in his life. The home he'd been looking for since he'd become a civilian again.

With her, he felt peace and purpose combine.

"I'm just saying, I don't take it all for granted. I hope I never take it for granted. I can't imagine my life without all of you in it."

Which wasn't the same thing as *I don't want to leave* or *I don't want to give this life up*. Her words cut through him, shattering the fantasy he'd been living in since she'd come into his life.

The urge to reassure her was automatic. "We aren't going anywhere."

But she might. Too much of her life had been controlled by someone else. When all this was over, when the world was open to her at last, she had every right to leave and explore it. Given Hamish's reaction to her identity, Ewan was coming to understand exactly how big a deal she actually was. He couldn't imagine her being happy and satisfied staying in his tiny village long-term. Certainly not continuing to work in his pub as a server. She was truly gifted, and she deserved the chance to get back to her music. To find the happiness that had been stripped away from her.

Needing some space to come to terms with that, he asked her the one thing guaranteed to grant it without raising alarm. "Will you play for me?"

Her lips curved into a delighted smile. "A private concert?"

"Aye."

She pressed a fast kiss to his chest and rolled away, practically dancing her way to the violin. Ewan stayed where he was, watching her fuss with putting on the new strings, pausing only long enough to slip on the button-down shirt he'd worn to Sunday dinner at his parents'. When she finally drew the bow across the strings, she fairly glowed with joy.

The music flowed out of her, a sensual melody that echoed everything they'd just done, stroking senses, stoking his arousal. The full, rich sound filled the cabin, reaching straight into his chest and squeezing until he could barely breathe for wanting her.

This was what she was meant to do. Who she was meant to be. He couldn't be the one to hold her back after she'd fought so hard for her freedom. No matter how much it would kill him to watch this brave, beautiful woman he'd fallen in love with walk away.

As the last notes died, she lowered the violin, her eyes huge and dark, her chest heaving from exertion.

Ewan reached out for her. "Come back to bed."

Setting the instrument aside, she took his hand, and he pulled her in, rolled her beneath him. He wouldn't think of the after. Wouldn't waste time on the grief of what was to come. Now was for pleasure. He'd take this time with her, however much they had, and enjoy it. Committing it and her to memories that would keep him warm long after she'd left him behind.

## 14

"Still at it?"

At the sound of Ewan's voice, Isobel pulled her brain out of the music to find him in the kitchen lowering a bunch of fish into the sink. "Where did those come from?"

His lips twitched. "The river. I've been gone for over two hours."

And she hadn't even noticed. "Oh God, Ewan, I'm sorry. Why didn't you tell me? I'd have gone with you."

He scrubbed his hands. "You seemed to be in the zone. I didnae want to interrupt. The writing's going well, I take it?"

"The writing's going *amazing*. This is the third new song since we got here." This place, this man, inspired her. And maybe part of it was the prospect of finally being free of Paul and of being so out of reach, she didn't have to worry about the consequences. Yet, anyway. But she wasn't thinking about that. She was too buoyed by the high of inspiration.

A surge of joy drove her to her feet to twirl toward Ewan. Or try. Her muscles were stiff from inactivity, so she staggered, stumbling over her own feet.

But, of course, he caught her. He was great at that.

"How long has it been since you've moved?"

She linked her arms around his shoulders. "Uh… probably since whenever the last time was before you left."

Steadying her, he laced his hands at the small of her back. "At the risk of being dictatorial, you need a break. Are you where you can stop for a bit, or will that mess up your flow?"

Isobel waggled her eyebrows. "I'm always up for a break with you." Over the past week and a half, she'd learned he was a generous, enthusiastic, and inventive lover. She'd absolutely reaped the benefits. "What did you have in mind?"

His blue-grey eyes darkened. "Well, I wasnae thinking about that, but now you've put the idea in my head."

With a mock gasp, she curled her fingers into the hair at his nape. "The horror. Whatever will we do?"

He scooped her up, bride-style, and carted her toward the bed. "Have dessert first."

"You do have the best ideas." Inspired in a wholly different fashion, she nibbled along his throat and higher to lick the shell of his ear, delighting at the rumbling curse he uttered before tumbling them both onto the mattress.

She'd never tire of this. Never tire of him.

They were already halfway to naked, and her hand was inches from diving into his boxers to claim him when a phone rang. The sound was so unexpected she froze. "What…?"

"Satellite phone. I gave the number to Hamish so he could reach us."

"Oh."

Ewan scooted off the bed, rummaging in one of his bags and bringing out something that looked more like a walkie-talkie to her. "Hello? Aye, she's right here. Hang on. I'll put you on speaker." He punched another button. "Okay."

"Isobel?" Hamish's voice echoed off the stone wall.

"Yes, I'm here."

"I have news."

Feeling exposed, she reached for the shirt Ewan had stripped off and pulled it back over her head. "Lay it on me."

Ewan sank down beside her on the bed, linking his fingers with hers.

"First off, the certified letter was delivered last week, so Paul Burgette is officially no longer your representative, and he's aware of that fact."

She could imagine the rage and his absolute sense of impotence. He'd have taken it out on someone. "Have there been any reprisals from that?"

"Not to my knowledge. Right now, he's playing by the book. I put forth the request for the audit, which got about as far as I thought it would. Lots of dodging. I can keep pushing there, but it did exactly what I hoped it would do. I have a copy of the contract your mother signed."

"Really? That's great."

"Well, it's something."

"That doesnae sound like a great," Ewan observed.

"There's good news and bad news."

Isobel braced herself. "Bad news first."

"It's an incredibly predatory contract, and unfortunately, it is binding and enforceable. He's the one who owns the rights to your masters for everything you've recorded up to this point. He can do whatever he wants with those. Sell or license them to whomever he wishes."

Her heart sank. So she wasn't free after all. "That's it then. He's right. There's no way I can have a career in music."

"No, he's not. First off, he won't own anything you produce from this point forward. But you don't have to write off everything you've done before. Because you're the songwriter, you have some additional options I'd like to discuss with you when you get home."

Ewan wrapped an arm around her. "Is it safe to come home?Has there been any trouble since we've been gone?"

"We have no reason to think Burgette will be back."

"Back?" Isobel tightened her hold on Ewan's hand. "He's been to Glenlaig?"

"Oh, yes. You figured he'd see the video and track you down, and you were right."

He knew where she'd been. The idea that he could show up at any time left her cold inside. Her haven, her new life, was no longer safe. "What happened?"

"It was... interesting." But it was amusement rather than caution that laced Hamish's tone. "I think the others would rather explain that themselves when you get back. When should we expect you?"

Isobel met Ewan's gaze.

He'd asked her last week what she wanted when she was free. She hadn't had an answer for him then, but she'd been thinking about it. She wanted a normal life. The chance to make and keep real friends and to enjoy the found family she'd fallen into through him. She wanted to write new music, exploring new directions she'd been denied before, adding in all the emotionality and maturity she hadn't been brave enough to push for when Paul and her label had wanted more of the same. She wanted to go back to music on her own terms. No more massive, sold-out venues. No more endless touring. Maybe someday she'd want that again. But for now, she wanted to fall back in love with music the way she'd fallen in love with him.

And in order to have any of it, she had to go back.

She'd known, objectively, that they couldn't stay here forever. These past days had been a happy little honeymoon period. But Ewan couldn't take a permanent leave of absence from his business, and she, inevitably, had to face the consequences of finally separating from Paul, whatever that looked like. No matter how much it terrified her.

Ewan traced her temple, tucking a strand of hair behind her ear. "Tomorrow. It's too late to set out tonight, and there are things we need to wrap up here. I'll send an updated ETA when we have one."

Pitifully relieved to have one more night, she slumped against him, cuddling closer when his arm tightened around her.

"Understood. You've got a lot of people looking forward to seeing you both. Be safe."

Wrapped up in Ewan, it was easy to make that promise. "We will. And Hamish? Thank you."

"Any time. See you tomorrow."

Ewan hung up and tossed the phone aside. "You okay?"

She sighed, relaxing at the steady thump of his heart beneath her cheek. "I think so. It's a scary thing, reclaiming my life."

"You're not doing it alone."

"Which is the only reason I've gotten this far. I couldn't have done any of this without you."

His lips brushed her brow. "Then it's a good thing you dinna have to."

"Are you sure you want to do this?" Ewan knew where he fell on the matter, and it was not on the side of going to a family dinner at his pub and revealing Isobel's identity to everyone.

"They've earned the right to know. They went to all this trouble to protect me, and surely after all that, they've started to figure it out already. Wouldn't it be better to tell them myself?"

He only grunted in reply.

Not that he didn't trust his friends and family. Certainly, he did. As she'd said, they'd absolutely proven themselves. But it was another sign of how things were changing, and he was afraid of change. In the privacy of his own head, he could admit that. He was afraid of what came on the other side of her facing all this.

At the cabin, she'd been happy and relaxed. Truly unafraid for the first time since he'd known her. Seeing her with that violin in her hands, not only playing but composing music, had been humbling and awe-inspiring. She'd come alive, a vibrant joy shining out of every pore. And he'd fallen even more in love with her.

Ewan didn't want her to lose even a drop of that happiness, and he knew that no matter what the legalities said, Burgette would do anything he could to rob her of all of it. That simple fact kept him on edge as they rolled into the village and pulled into the carpark. He saw nothing and no one out of the ordinary for mid-afternoon on a weekday, but he kept his head on a swivel as he hustled Isobel into the pub through the back door.

Dom was the first to spot them. His smile spread wide. "There's our girl! It's good to have you back."

Isobel beamed at him and moved into his open arms for a hug. "It's good to be back."

Laura came hurrying down the hall to get in on the hugs. "There she is. And don't you look wonderful? The time away was good for you." She flicked an amused gaze at him. "Both of you."

Ewan felt his ears heat. Was it that obvious they'd been sleeping together?

He brought up the rear as they all moved into the main part of the pub. With a practiced eye, he assessed the crowd, seeing no one who wasn't a local among the twenty or so patrons spread through the room. A few of them noticed them and called out greetings to him and to Isobel. A little of his wariness ebbed. Jason was on the stick at the bar, and both Isla and Zo worked the tables with their usual efficiency.

Ciara emerged from the private party room. "You're back!" She bolted across the room to wrap Isobel in a hug.

"I am. I hear there was some... excitement?"

His sister pursed her lips. "You could say that. Come on. Everybody's in here."

Everybody turned out to be both his cousins, their significant others, Charlotte and Malcolm, Angus and Munro, and Hamish. As Isobel made the rounds for more hugs, Ewan was pleased to note how much easier she was with the affection than she had been. It was yet another sign that she was relaxing and settling here. All the more reason to do whatever he could to protect this for her.

He waited until they'd all made their orders, then shut the door. "Tell me about Burgette. What happened?"

Ciara leaned back in her chair. "So this posh arsehole shows up asking about Callie McLean—"

Isobel frowned. "Who?"

"That's the name we came up with for the social media persona to attach to the video," Kyla explained.

"Right, so we told them you were a competitor for the Battle of the Bands."

Connor picked up the thread. "He said that was grand, that he was looking for you to offer representation. That he was some hotshot in the music industry."

"He would do that," Isobel muttered.

"So we gave him the contact information we had—which was falsified, of course—and we sent him on down to Wales for a wild goose chase." Ciara looked smug. "We figured the further we could get him from here, the better."

Sophie leaned into Connor's arm. "He did ask around the village, but everyone gave him some variation of that same story, so there's no reason to think he'll be back."

These people weren't tacticians. Ewan wasn't sure Burgette would be put off that easily, but at the same time, he approved of the fact that they'd all collectively banded together to fuck with him. At the very least, they'd likely bought a little more time for Hamish to do his thing.

Isobel looked around the table. "Thank you—all of you—for your efforts." She took a breath, and Ewan knew this was the end of her relative anonymity. "I feel like it's time to tell you what all of this is actually about."

"You mean the fact that you're Elizabeth Duncan?" Kyla asked.

Isobel blinked. "How did you—"

Raleigh waved away her shock. "It's all over the comment thread on the video. People think you're pulling a Chris Gaines."

"A what now?"

"Oh, back in the late nineties, country star Garth Brooks came up with this whole other persona, Chris Gaines, and put out an alternative rock album," Charlotte explained. "It was something to do with a movie that never got made. Anyway, the point is, your fans know it's you. They think the whole thing is some kind of publicity stunt."

Some of the color drained from Isobel's cheeks. "It's not. God, I hope you don't think I've been hanging out here for all these weeks, using everybody—"

Munro patted her hand. "Nobody thinks that, love."

She nodded, her shoulders relaxing. "I don't want to get into the specifics of why I ran, but just know that he's... not a good man. And he's no longer my agent. I'm not sure exactly what that means for me, because he owns the rights to all my music." She looked to Hamish. "You said you had another idea about that?"

"I do. Do I have your permission to speak freely in front of everyone?"

"Go ahead. Maybe they'll have some ideas, too."

"So predatory contracts are not, unfortunately, rare in the music industry. But there is legal precedent for you, as the songwriter of record, to do something about it. The songs themselves are your intellectual property. You can re-record them, so long as you change them a little, give them some new twist or spin, then re-release them. That's what Taylor Swift has done."

"But that doesn't supersede his ownership of the previous masters. How does re-recording help?"

"Because you'd own the new masters. What's happened with Swift is that she's been very public about what she's doing, why she's doing it. Her fans are diehard supportive of her, so they're flocking to purchase and listen to the new recordings. And radio stations and other distribution centers are vowing only to play the new versions, so she's effectively undercutting the people who own the rights to those original recordings. You could do the same thing."

Those fascinating eyes lit with triumph. "Oh, that's *perfect!*"

"People have already figured out the fake social media profile we set up was you," Kyla said. "They love the music itself. It's got a different sound than the other stuff you've put out. If you can bring that new direction to your re-recordings, fans will follow. You have the platform."

The idea clearly intrigued her. "You're sure there's no non-compete clause or something?"

"Have you signed anything beyond the original agreement?" Hamish asked.

"No."

"Then, no. There's not. Likely because Burgette has been able to control you all this time, and he didn't think it was necessary. He never expected you to walk."

She settled back in her chair. "The rerecording wouldn't be a big deal. Certainly, I can create new arrangements of all of it.

But how to get the word out about it? I don't have control of my social media channels."

"Well, you've got the ones we created," Sophie pointed out. "The followers have been racking up. You could easily come clean, as it were, and take ownership of those."

"It's a start, for sure."

"Oh, oh! I have an idea." Ciara rose and began to pace. "Hear me out. You should publicly announce this. Same as Taylor did. Tell your fans what you're doing and why. The public loves to get outraged on behalf of people who've been screwed over. And this weekend's Highland Games are the ideal place to kick it off. You should play with the winners from the Battle of the Bands."

"I'm not taking over their show. That's not fair to any of them."

"There's not a one among them who'd object to playing with you. Do you have any idea how much extra publicity that would buy for them? And I'm not saying you should take over. Just use it as a platform to get the word out."

Isobel clapped her hands together, grinning. "I *love* it."

Ewan hated it. He didn't want to rain on Isobel's fresh enthusiasm, but he had to point out what none of the rest of them had considered. "Are you sure you want to do that? Because it's a major security risk. There will be people everywhere and a lot of elements we willnae be able to control."

"That's exactly why it's a good idea. Paul's not going to try anything in front of all those people. That would just make him look bad, and he's nothing if not aware of the optics. I can't keep hiding away forever. I have to take the steps to get my life back, and it sounds like this is a solid first step."

There was an eagerness underlying her words that worried him. He hadn't forgotten what happened to the cellist. Burgette wasn't going to just bow out gracefully, and he'd already proved a willingness to hire out the unethical. What happened if he sent someone after Isobel? Someone to destroy the thing that mattered most to her? Over the past couple of weeks, Ewan had come to understand how much music truly meant to her. If she lost the ability to play, it would kill her.

But how could he bring that up to her and extinguish that light in her eyes? How could he stop her from taking the steps to regain the life that was rightfully hers?

He swallowed down his objections and vowed he'd do whatever he had to in order to make sure she was safe.

"Okay, if that's what you want to do, we'll make it happen."

## 15

"Go! Go! Go! Pull!" Isobel jumped and shouted along with the rest of the crowd. On the field, Connor, Raleigh, Malcolm, and a whole host of men she didn't know were pitted against each other in teams of fifteen on either side of a massive rope playing the most testosterone fueled game of tug of war she'd ever seen.

Ewan should've been down there with them. Instead, his head was on a swivel, scanning everyone and everything, braced for action. Though he hadn't outright said it, she knew he thought this was a bad idea. She'd learned to read him and his silences. But he hadn't tried to stop her, and she appreciated that more than she could say. After years of having someone else call the shots, being in control was a high she hadn't expected. She had to believe this was the right first step. For the first time, with the help of all her new family and friends, she believed she truly would get her life back.

Seeing the comments and all the support pouring in on social media for Callie McLean, even though she hadn't posted as herself yet, had been overwhelming in the best possible way. She regretted not having taken more ownership of her fandom in the past, and she was actually looking forward to taking control of her music and of her career in a way that she'd never done before.

No announcement had been made publicly about what would be happening later that night. While there was music throughout the day, the festival coordinators had elected to save the best for last, with the first-place winner of the Battle of the Bands as the headliners. Celtic Hearts, Soairse's band, was slated to perform after the last of the games, and all eyes would be on the stage. Isobel had spoken with them about sliding in as part of their set, and as Ciara had predicted, they were psyched to have her. They were even scrambling to learn one of the new songs she'd written out at the cabin.

She felt a fizz and pop in her blood at the prospect of performing again. After two months away from the stage, she loved the idea of coming back to it here. The Glenlaig Highland Games were a casual outdoor venue. Everywhere around her were families, couples, and friends. The entire atmosphere was one of relaxed enjoyment, without an ounce of pretension. And she knew a big portion of the audience. When was the last time she'd performed for a group who wasn't entirely made up of strangers?

In a way, that made the prospect of this announcement easier. Making it in front of friends. Members of the community. People who actually cared about her. Maybe not everyone would, but she could handle that. She wasn't afraid of the small, of the starting over. Because it would finally be *her* way.

The crowd was a mix of cheers and groans as Connor, Raleigh, and Hamish's team successfully dragged their competitors over the line.

Beside her, Ciara made noises of admiration under her breath. "That never gets old. All those braw kilted lads with their muscly thighs. Mmm."

Isobel glanced over at Ewan, looking utterly delicious in his own kilt. "You're not wrong." He tended toward jeans and t-shirts at the pub. He still wore one of the t-shirts that stretched over his formidable muscles, but the addition of the kilt had inspired a whole host of fantasies. Maybe it was the idea that he could have her against a wall and be inside her in a matter of seconds. The idea of it had her squeezing her thighs together.

"Put that look away," he murmured.

She adopted an expression of total innocence. "What?"

"You ken what. There are too many people here."

"More's the pity."

He growled at her, and she couldn't hold back the grin. At least until she noticed Bonnie noticing and grinning even wider. Ewan's mother seemed even more delighted with her since they'd returned from the cabin. The pair of them might as well have taken a billboard out announcing they were sleeping together. Everyone seemed to know. Not that anyone had said anything directly. It had been all sly winks and smiles. Everyone seemed genuinely happy they were together, which was its own kind of welcome. Isobel appreciated that. Not that she and Ewan had defined what they were. They just seemed to have fallen into being... whatever they were. They fit. With so many other things up in the air, she appreciated *not* having to discuss and label their relationship. It was nice to simply accept that they were on the same page.

Sliding her arm through his, she pulled him into a stroll. "Let's walk. I need to visit the loo."

Trailed by the rest of his family, who were acting as an informal guard for the day, they began to stroll the perimeter of the field, toward the booths of food and stalls selling everything from Nessie plushies to tartans to forged weapons. Connor had brought out what seemed like a whole armory's worth of weaponry he'd made at Ardinmuir Ironworks. She'd been fascinated to see his work as a blacksmith, and he'd promised to give her a tour sometime.

Out on the grass, event staff and competitors began to prepare for the caber toss.

Seeing Ewan's glance in that direction, she asked, "Have you ever competed in the games?"

James beamed with pride. "Oh, aye. He won the hammer throw last year. Was a hell of a thing to watch."

"And then there was the sword fighting demonstration," Ciara added.

More than curious, Isobel slid a glance up at him. "Sword fighting demonstration?"

"Aye. I've got training in a multitude of weapons, so the organizers asked me to do a demonstration. Connor and I enacted a duel. It was verra popular."

She imagined him in full regalia, with that warrior's body and a sword and felt herself heat. "I bet it was."

"He was signed up for the games this year, too, but pulled out," Bonnie added.

Guilt struck. He'd cancelled because of her.

Ewan laid a hand over hers on his arm and squeezed. "I'm where I want to be."

Before she could reply, someone screamed.

In an instant, he wrapped around her, using himself as a shield, even as he searched for the source of the threat.

"Help! We need a doctor!"

The disturbance was at the edge of the field.

"Where's Dr. Albright?" Ewan called over the melee.

"It *is* Dr. Albright! Oh, God, he's not breathing."

"Where the bloody hell is the ambulance?"

"They got called out!" someone shouted.

Isobel had only met the village doctor once. A hale and hearty man in his late sixties, with a big laugh and kind eyes, she knew he was the only doctor in town. She squeezed Ewan's arm. "You have medical training. You should help."

When he hesitated, she squeezed again. "I'm fine. I'm right here with your family. He needs whatever help he can get."

With a short nod, he released her and cut through the crowd to the circle gathered around a prone form. The crowd parted, and he dropped to his knees in the grass beside the old man. They all watched as he checked for a pulse and then began CPR. Despite the hundreds of people present, everything had gone silent, waiting, but for the older woman sobbing nearby. Isobel wondered if that was the doctor's wife.

"I called 999. Help is being dispatched, but it's going to take time to get here."

Ewan just nodded, not breaking rhythm.

Someone ran over from the medical tent with a portable defibrillator, and Isobel felt faint. It wasn't the same as her mother, and yet... the crowd of people, the body prone on the ground...

"I hate to step away, but I really need to use the loo," she murmured to Bonnie. "I'll be right back."

James straightened, dividing his attention between Isobel and the man on the ground. "Oh, I'll come with you."

"No, stay here near your friend. It's twenty feet. I'll be right there. I'm just going to run over, and I'll be right back."

She slipped away, weaving through the still crowd and right to the row of portaloos set at the corner between the field where the events were being held and the start of the vendor tents. Just a couple of minutes. She just needed a couple minutes and to not see them trying to shock Dr. Albright back to life. And she really did need to go. She closed herself inside and did her business.

Outside, the crowd didn't make a sound. That couldn't be a good thing.

*Please let him be okay. Please let him be okay.*

The moment she stepped outside, her eyes combed through the people clustered around where the doctor lay on the ground. But before she could determine what was happening, a hand covered her mouth, and an arm hauled her roughly back against a taller form.

Her heart tripped as an all too familiar cold voice murmured, "Did you think you could get away from me that easily?"

RELIEF COURSED through Ewan as he felt the faint bump of life beneath his fingers. Two rounds with the AED, but they'd gotten him back. For now. He knew they weren't out of the woods yet, but the gathered crowd needed some sort of news. "We've got a pulse!"

At the edge of the circle, Doc's wife, Loreena, sank to her knees. "Oh, thank God."

As cheers echoed around him, Ewan bent low. "C'mon, old man. Dinna leave us now. You've still got work to do."

The mood palpably lifted, and he hoped like hell it continued to be justified. In the distance, he finally heard the siren of the ambulance returning. Thank God.

Fingers still monitoring the thready pulse, he eased back, finally tearing his gaze away from Doc Albright to check on Isobel. When she wasn't where he'd left her, he automatically began scanning, searching for his family. Not spotting them either, he frowned. Where were they?

"Excuse me. Coming through."

The paramedics hustled through the crowd, their medical bags bumping against their backs and hips. Ewan gave way so they could kneel on either side.

"What happened?"

As succinctly as possible, he told them, answering questions about how long Doc had been without a pulse, how long he'd done compressions, and the use of the AED to shock his heart.

"We'll take it from here. Does anyone know his medical history?"

"I do." Loreena stepped forward. "I'm his wife."

Relieved to turn the situation over, Ewan dove into the throngs, accepting praise and slaps on the shoulder as he headed toward where he'd last seen everyone. He finally spotted his mother, pale-faced, hands knit together, several rows back from the action.

"Doc Albright's a fighter. We got a pulse back. He's got a good chance." It was the most comfort he could offer with certainty. "Where's Isobel?"

Her blue-grey eyes shone with distress. "We canna find her."

Ewan's gut clenched. "What do you mean you canna find her? Where did she go?" Before Bonnie even began to speak again, he went on alert, looking for that familiar flash of dark hair.

"She went to the loo. She was just over there." Bonnie pointed to where a short line of people was rotating in and out.

"How long?" he demanded.

"Your da offered to go with her, but he was worried about Peter—"

"How long?" Ewan repeated, urgency beating in his blood.

"Maybe ten minutes. When she didn't come back in a couple of minutes, James and Ciara went to look for her."

But they hadn't come back either. Ewan wasn't worried about them. Burgette wouldn't know them and had no reason to get them involved. No, his focus would be entirely on Isobel.

Ewan jogged over to the row of portaloos, circling around them, analyzing the ground. With all the foot traffic, it was impossible to determine whether the turf showed signs of a struggle. There probably hadn't been one. Certainly, the crowd had been quiet enough someone would've heard and noticed. But Isobel wouldn't go off on her own. If she'd truly just gone to use the loo, she'd have come back by now.

Dread pooled in Ewan's chest as he analyzed faces, searching for the one he needed among all the strangers. He'd known this was a huge security risk. He never should have agreed to let her come. More, he should never have left her alone. And yet, how could he have left Doc Albright when he had the skills to help?

Self-recrimination would have to wait. He needed to act now. If Burgette had her himself, or if he'd sent someone after her, they wouldn't be sticking around, and they had a solid lead.

By the field, the crowd was parting to allow the ambulance to back up near the patient. It was the only vehicle nearby. Public parking for the event was a full kilometer away as the crow flew. Longer by the farm road that most had walked to get here. She wouldn't have gone willingly, so either a weapon of some sort was involved or she'd been incapacitated somehow. Either way, they wouldn't be on the road. Too many prospective witnesses who could raise the alarm.

He started toward the woods, then hesitated. What if he was wrong? What if Burgette had come in some other way? Except, how could he? He wasn't a local and didn't know the area. Nothing in the profile Conway had put together on him indicated he was the sort to have done proper reconnaissance when he'd been here before. He couldn't have predicted Doc's heart attack. This was a crime of opportunity. That meant he'd be moving fast and risking mistakes.

Ciara ran up, cheeks pale despite her clear exertion. "We can't find Isobel!"

James was right behind, looking absolutely sick. "I only took my eyes off her for a couple of minutes. I'm so sorry."

"Later," Ewan snapped. "Find Hamish, Malcolm, and the

others. Get an announcement on the loudspeaker. Get every-fucking-body in Glenlaig who kens her searching. I'm headed through the woods to the carpark. Send someone else up the road."

Connor strode up, a sword and shield from his booth strapped to his back. His brows were knit in concern. "What's going on?"

"Isobel's gone. We have to assume Burgette took her. She wouldn't have left on her own."

"I'll help look."

They moved toward the woods, searching for any sign she'd passed this way. Even before the announcement was made, Ewan heard the news begin to spread as those who'd overheard told someone else. Yes, there were a multitude of strangers here, but the villagers still made up the majority of attendees, and most of them knew Isobel by now.

Archie ran up. "I found this." He held out a silver necklace in a trembling hand. The thistle charm glinted in the afternoon sun. "Isn't it Isobel's?"

Grim purpose settled over him. "Aye. Where, lad?"

Archie led him over to the edge of the forest and here Ewan saw what he'd been looking for. The scuff of feet. Signs, not so much of a struggle, but of someone trying to slow down. A few meters in, the trees were so thick, no one down by the games would be able to see anyone who'd disappeared.

"Where do you want me?" Connor asked.

"Circle around by the road. And just in case, assume he's armed. She wouldn't have gone willingly."

Connor nodded and took off the broadsword and targe, handing both over. Ewan tested the weight of the weapon in his hand and found the perfect balance. "How sharp is this?"

Connor picked up another. "This blade isn't for demonstration. It'll cut."

Ewan hoped it didn't come to that. "Meet you around in the

parking lot. And be careful. Dinna engage. You've got a wedding to be around for."

"We'll get her back, Cousin."

If they didn't, Ewan would be bringing a full-scale war to Burgette's doorstep.

Armed, he rushed back toward the treeline. Drawing on all his years of training and missions, he slipped into the green darkness and began to hunt.

## 16

Clammy sweat slid down Isobel's spine, a contrast to the cold steel of the knife pressed against her back. At least, she hoped it was sweat and not blood. He'd pricked her at least once in urging her away.

The jab of it against her back had been the only thing keeping her from fighting back and making some kind of scene to draw attention. He'd kept her close, leading her through the crowd as he had so many times before, and Isobel felt herself wanting to shrink, to acquiesce. To give in.

But she wasn't that woman anymore. She'd found her spine. Her place. Her people. And he had no more power than what she gave him.

Unfortunately, that was still far more than she liked as they marched through the forest. She'd thought perhaps his hold might slacken once they were out of view and that there might be an opportunity to slip away from him. But his hand still had her upper arm in a vise grip, and he still used the threat of the knife and his bigger bulk to steer her.

At least she'd managed to drop her necklace. Hopefully, someone would find it.

*Oh, please let someone find it.*

"Where are you taking me?"

"That's not your concern. You ungrateful brat. Do you have any idea what you've put me through the last two months? How many concerts were cancelled? How many excuses I had to make for you, because you decided to be irresponsible?"

The apology rose to her lips, but she didn't let it fall.

"It's going to take me a long time to forgive you, Elizabeth. But you can still fix this. You've had your little vacation. It's time for you to get back to work. We can get the tour stops rescheduled—"

He was completely insane if he thought she was doing any of that. And yet she knew if he'd come so far as to kidnap her at knifepoint, arguing with him might push him over some edge.

As long as they were on foot, they weren't that far from the games. Someone would notice her missing when she didn't come back. Ewan would be notified. He'd find her. She just needed to buy some time.

Her sense of direction wasn't the best, but she was reasonably sure the secondary field that had been turned into a carpark for the games was in this direction. If Paul got her to a vehicle and managed to get her to some other location, it would make it that much harder to find her. So, she needed to keep them from getting to a vehicle. She began dragging her feet, pretending to stumble. Then her foot caught on a root, and she didn't have to fake it.

Paul's vicious grip kept her upright. "Keep moving."

She knew this tone. Knew how to placate. Her voice held a legitimate quaver when she spoke. "I... I'm sorry, Paul."

"You're bloody well right, you're sorry. Cost me all that time and effort. Made me look like a fool. And you thought you could *fire* me? *Me?* How dare you, Elizabeth. Honestly. You'd have nothing without me. I made you the musician you are."

Temper sparked. "My father made me the musician I am."

"Oh, your father. The sainted Padrig Donnchadh, who was too stupid to cash in on the talent right under his nose."

"My father understood there were more important things than money."

"Which proves how much of a fool he truly was. Money is power. And I hold all the power, Elizabeth." To emphasize the point, he pressed the knife, just a little, into her back.

Isobel arched away from the blade. "Stop! You're hurting me."

"I'll do worse than that if you don't cooperate."

They were reaching the edge of the woods. Through the trees, she could see row upon row of cars. She had no idea which one was his, but she knew she was out of time. She'd have to fight him, somehow.

Spotting a gnarled root crossing their path, she deliberately hooked her toes, shifting her weight hard enough that it sent her sprawling, jerking her arm out of his grip.

"Get up, you clumsy idiot."

Isobel curled her hands into the earth, gripping fistfuls, and as she pushed to her feet, she flung them both at his face.

Paul swore, slashing toward her with the knife. She threw herself back, but found her escape blocked by the tight-knit branches of the trees. In horror, she watched the blade slicing down, down, down...

A blood-curdling roar sounded. A blur of plaid slid in front of her.

*Ewan!*

Isobel screamed because there was no way the knife wouldn't hit him.

But there was a solid *thunk* as the blade bounced off of something. Then Ewan was moving forward, swinging a... holy shite! That was a sword. He drove Paul back four stumbling steps, effectively parrying every sloppy strike of the knife with a shield before handily disarming him and bashing the shield against his head.

Paul crumpled like a rag doll.

Ewan kicked the knife well out of reach, then turned to her, chest heaving, eyes ablaze. "Are you all right? Did he hurt you? Christ, you're bleeding."

He closed the distance between them and dropped the sword and shield, wrapping those strong arms around her so tight she was crushed to his chest.

Isobel just held on.

"No. No, I'm okay. Just scared. He only nicked me." As the reality of what had almost happened sank in, so too did the shakes. "Oh God. Oh God. Ewan."

"It's okay. I've got you. You're safe."

"I knew you'd come for me."

"Always."

She pulled back to look up at him in wonder. "You came with a *sword*."

He shrugged. "It's what was available."

A siren sounded in the distance.

"That'll be the police. Good. Someone would've notified them."

From where he lay on the ground several feet away, Paul began to groan. Ewan released her. Using his foot to kick the sword back up into his hand, he crossed over, laying the tip of the blade against the hollow of Paul's throat, so the first thing her former manager saw when he roused was more than six feet of livid Highlander.

His eyes wheeled as he looked for any kind of weapon or help.

Ewan just pressed the blade forward a millimeter. "Give me a reason."

"I'll give you one not to. You're standing up with me at my

wedding, Cousin. Dinna do something that'll end you up in jail." Similarly armed, Connor strode through the trees.

"They'd have to find the body first." Ewan muttered.

The complete loss of color from Paul's face was more than gratifying.

Another man, dressed in a police uniform, was a dozen feet behind. "I'll pretend I didnae hear that. You want to step back now?"

"Want is a strong word," Ewan drawled.

The officer dangled handcuffs. "I've got this, lad."

Ewan stepped back, returning to pull her into his arms as she heard the sweetest words.

"You're under arrest for attempted kidnapping…"

IT WAS NEARING midnight by the time Ewan and Isobel made it home. What had been intended as a piggyback performance of a few songs with Celtic Hearts had turned into a true Elizabeth Duncan concert, keeping the crowd—including Ewan—enthralled for two full hours past the intended closing out of the Highland Games. She'd been positively electric, glowing with an inner fire that wouldn't be denied. There'd been a celebratory air around the whole affair in the wake of her identity reveal. And the announcement that she'd be re-recording her albums and releasing them to compete with the ones she was denied the chance to own. Not a soul had wanted to stop it.

Havoc greeted them both with full-body wriggles of ecstasy, soaking up love before bolting into the darkness to do his business. He was back a minute later, leaping onto the couch to get closer to Isobel. She slumped against the arm of the couch, a tired smile on her face as she buried her fingers in the ruff around Havoc's neck, scratching until he moaned in canine delight.

How could she look so right exactly here, like this, and also perfect on stage? It was almost as if she were two different women, and Ewan didn't entirely know what to do with that.

"How do you feel?"

Pressing a kiss to Havoc's head, she lifted her arms overhead and stretched. "I feel pretty fantastic. Shattered, but fantastic."

"You looked fantastic up there on that stage. I thought I understood when I saw you play at the pub, and again all that time at the cabin. But I didnae have a clue. Seeing you like that, lighting up that audience, was incredible. You're incredible." And it had brought home, in a very real way, exactly what she'd walked away from and exactly how far this life in Glenlaig was from her reality. This was what she'd done for half her life. It was what she was so clearly meant to do.

Shoving away from the sofa, she slid her arms around his neck. "You were pretty incredible today, too. Thanks for rescuing me."

Ewan shuddered, pulling her closer. "Took ten years off my life when I saw him coming at you with that knife."

"I'm pretty sure I'll be having nightmares about it for a good long while, but you charged straight in like the hero of a historical romance novel. I'll never forget the sight of you with that sword and shield. That'll be in my dreams for a long time, too."

"Targe," he corrected. "That particular kind of shield is a targe." Guilt continued to twist like a dirk between his ribs as he considered what could've happened if he hadn't made it in time. He knew all too well the damage a blade could do to human flesh. "I'm sorry he ever managed to get to you. I promised he wouldn't. I promised you'd be safe. I should never have left your side in the first place."

"Of course you should. You couldn't leave Dr. Albright. Has there been any word on his condition?"

"He's stable. They're predicting he'll make a full recovery, though he willnae be able to keep pushing as much as he has been, so that'll light a fire under the village council to work on truly finding someone to join his practice, which will make his wife happy."

"Add to that the fact that the magistrate denied Paul bail, and it seems like an all-around good ending to what could have been a truly terrible day."

Ewan stroked the hair back from her face. "You're finally free."

"It seems I am. I could never have done any of this without you."

From the very beginning, he'd wanted to save her. Wanted to give her a stable foundation she'd clearly never had. And he'd done that. But he hadn't known what he'd find with her. Hadn't known how she'd stabilize his own world. Hadn't known she could never stay.

He knew it now. Tonight's concert had proved beyond the shadow of a doubt that sharing and performing music was what she was meant to do. She'd been put on this earth to do so much more than serve at his pub. He'd promised himself that he wouldn't fight this. That he'd let her go when the time came, because she deserved the chance to go back to that life without all the restrictions she'd lived with before. Without being manipulated by what he wanted. He never wanted to do anything to make her feel small.

So he knew the end was coming. The media would've gotten wind of Elizabeth Duncan's return by now. Social media was already blowing up with videos of tonight's performance. And she'd need to get started on all those new recordings. Her time in the shadows was over, and that big, beautiful life was waiting.

But Ewan was going to take tonight. For himself. For her. If their time together was over, he'd make sure they both remembered it.

Hooking a finger beneath her chin, he tipped up that lovely

face and laid his lips over hers in a long, drugging kiss. With a sigh, she melted against him, all her softness molding against all his hardness. So often they'd been driven by the want, the need, rushing toward ecstasy. But not now. Now he wanted them both steeped in pleasure.

Ewan wasn't a dancer, but with her pliant in his arms, he began to circle them down the hall and into his bedroom, to the bed she'd shared since they'd returned to the village. The bed that would feel too empty without her. But he wouldn't think about that now. Not while she was still here. Not while she was still his.

He didn't bother with the lights, just undressed her in the pale shafts of moonlight that spilled in from the windows. Her hands skimmed over him, stripping off his t-shirt, unbuckling his kilt until it dropped to the floor. Wrapping his arms around her, he sank back on the bed, immediately rolling to take her mouth. Everything about her opened to him, her tongue seeking his, her legs parting. Ewan wanted to simply slide into her and lose himself. But not yet. Wedging a thigh against her center, he brought his hands to her breasts and began to drive her up. Her hips rose and fell, seeking the friction she needed against his leg.

Every whimper, every moan she made, he committed to memory. And when she began to gasp, "Need you. Ewan, please," he slipped a hand between them to send her tumbling over the edge.

She was still quaking when he ranged himself over her, but she reached up, framing his face and drawing him down, drawing him in. On a reverent curse, he sank inside her, feeling that exquisite heat wrap around him, claiming him body and soul as effectively as she'd claimed his heart.

*I love you.* The words trembled on his tongue, poised to spill out.

He couldn't tell her. Wouldn't use his feelings to sway her

away from what she needed to do. But he'd show her in this moment how much he loved her.

They moved together in a mating both familiar and miraculous, their bodies finding an unhurried rhythm. Sweat slicked his skin with the effort of maintaining the exquisitely torturous pace as they slowly rose together. With each stroke, he managed to sink just a little deeper, until at last he hit that spot deep inside that had her throwing back her head to moan, "Oh, God, more."

Pressing back one knee, he gave her what she wanted, sinking to the hilt.

Isobel's arms and free leg wrapped around him. "Stay. Please, just stay."

It was what he wanted to say to her. What he'd never say to her.

But he told her with his body, over and over, until that wave of thick pleasure crested and she broke around him, crying out his name. He held on with everything he had, until the pulsing of her release pulled him over behind her, and he spilled out everything he felt, everything he was.

Everything but the words that would keep her from leaving.

## 17

The only thing better than a lazy morning after a night of truly excellent sex was spending more of that morning back in bed. As Isobel lingered over a second cup of tea and cuddled Havoc on the sofa, she wondered whether she could convince Ewan to finish his workout in much more enjoyable, sweaty ways. Last night had been incredible. Maybe it had been the relief. Maybe the high of finally being able to perform again. Maybe it would just keep getting better every time. She couldn't find a thing wrong with that.

A knock on the door interrupted her contemplation. Havoc leapt down and shot toward the front door. Isobel unfolded and followed, grateful she'd put on something other than one of Ewan's shirts when she'd gotten up this morning.

Hamish stood on the front stoop, a long box under his arm. "Good morning. Sorry to disturb you. I had some news."

"Of course. Come in."

Ewan emerged from the hall. "What's wrong?"

"Nothing. The police searched Paul Burgette's lodgings.

He'd rented a room at an inn over in Duntyre. They found this." Hamish set the box on the kitchen table and opened it.

Isobel cried out, automatically reaching for the familiar leather case. She unzipped it, holding her breath as she lifted the lid, half terrified of what she'd find inside. But the violin was as she'd left it, quietly waiting to be played again. She trailed her fingers over the satin finish of the wood. "I don't know what I thought happened to it after I left. I guess a part of me assumed he might destroy it out of anger."

"Seems not. I thought you'd want it back."

Isobel flattened her hand against the instrument that was, in many ways, her heart and felt tears stream down her cheeks. "It's the last thing I have left of my father. Thank you."

"Of course. But that's not the only reason I came by. As your current representative, my inbox and phone have been blowing up. Last night's announcement and the performance has definitely gone viral. Multiple media outlets have reached out requesting interviews. Until you get further representation, I'm happy to continue to act on your behalf. I just need you to tell me how you'd like me to handle it."

"I appreciate it." She wiped at the tears. "I've got no interest in talking to the press. Not yet, anyway."

"Official line for now is no comment. Got it. Your current record label also wants to speak with you, and there are inquiries from two others."

"Already?" She'd thought she'd have a little more time before she had to make these kinds of decisions.

Hamish shrugged. "It's big news."

The thought of having to handle all this so quickly had a headache beginning to bloom at her temples. But she could at least make one immediate decision. "I won't be recording anything else with my current label. I'm not inclined to want to work with others, either, but I recognize that's likely premature without at least seeing what terms they're offering."

"I'll notify your current label. If they have any business to discuss regarding your current contractual obligations, they can send all that through me. There's likely going to be something relating to the remaining tour schedule. As to the others, shall I have them commit their offers in writing for your later review?"

"That sounds perfect."

"Excellent. And certainly, I'll review any prospective contracts to ensure you don't get caught up in something problematic again."

"I really appreciate it, Hamish. Thank you."

He rose. "I won't keep you. I know you've got things to do. But I also want to remind you... you hold the cards here. All these people can push as much as they want. It doesn't mean you have to let them."

She blew out a breath. "I absolutely needed to hear that."

A smile curved Hamish's lips. "Thought you might. I'll be in touch."

When he'd gone, Isobel sank back on the couch. "You're awfully quiet."

"None of that required my input." There was something odd in Ewan's matter-of-fact tone that she couldn't quite put her finger on.

Brushing away that frisson of worry, she admitted, "I'm not used to it requiring mine. I'm glad to be rid of Paul, but it's a whole new experience, being responsible for everything myself."

"You'll learn." Again, there was something... wrong in how he'd said it. The statement didn't sound like confidence. It sounded almost dismissive. But that couldn't be right.

Isobel realized he'd already changed out of his workout clothes and into his habitual work uniform of jeans and a t-shirt. "Are you getting ready to go into the pub?"

"Aye."

Damn. She must've lost track of time. "Oh, I'll go get ready.

Are you going in to check on things with a plan to work tonight or do you plan to work on through the afternoon?"

"I'm working through. There's no need for you to change. I didnae put you on the schedule."

After everything she'd been through, she supposed it did seem like she could use a day off to recover. But she didn't want to kick around here alone. "That's sweet, but really, I'm fine. I'm perfectly capable of working. And I've already been off all that time while we were away. This is what you pay me for."

"You and I both know you dinna actually need this job. The whole reason for it is over now. We've done what we set out to do. You're safe. Burgette is done, so you're free to go back to your normal life. There's nothing keeping you here."

Too stunned to speak, Isobel could only stare. Nothing keeping her here? What about him? What about them? She hadn't given any thought to leaving for weeks. Not because she couldn't fathom what having the freedom to do that might look like, but because she didn't want to. She'd thought they were on the same page. That he was happy with the life they'd been building together.

That he was as in love with her as she was with them.

But he hadn't said the words. And as he stared at her with flat eyes that had gone more grey than blue, she realized that she'd been a naïve fool. He'd never meant for it to be anything long term. She'd been a job. A mission. A temporary distraction.

*Quit your disasterizing. You can't have been that wrong about him.*

"You hired me for a reason. You needed the extra coverage for the summer season."

"I hired you because you needed a job. I think it's been adequately proven over the past couple of weeks that we've got it covered. Seriously, you're free to go. I ken you've got a lot of do."

*I want you to go*. They weren't the precise words he'd said, but his meaning was clear enough.

"I see." Except she didn't. Not really. How could he have made love to her so beautifully last night and today be telling her to leave?

He scooped up his keys from the bowl on the table. "I need to get to work."

Without her.

Isobel wanted to argue. But what more could she say? He'd made his position clear. He didn't want her help at the pub. He didn't seem to want her here at all anymore. She had no idea where she'd go or what she'd do, but she'd clearly outstayed her welcome.

Wrapping the tattered scraps of her pride around her splintered heart, she straightened. "Then I guess I'm going to go pack."

"Best bloody concert I've ever been to."

"And to think that's our Isobel. Such a sweet thing. What do you suppose she'll do next?"

A headache clawed at Ewan's skull as his patrons continued to talk about last night's show. He'd known they'd be discussing it. The reveal of her identity was the biggest news to hit Glenlaig since... well, Connor and Sophie's engagement and Kyla and Raleigh's wedding before that. People would be talking about it for weeks. Months. Years.

Rather than throw a chair, he prowled down the hall and shut himself into his office. Five minutes. Just five bloody minutes of quiet, so he could ache in peace.

She hadn't fought him. Hadn't made more than a token argument about the job. That was proof he'd done the right thing, even though it felt as if he were bleeding from an open chest wound.

She'd said she'd be packing, so maybe she'd even be gone before he got home. That would be better. No protracted good-bye. No risk of his resolve breaking.

Then again, she still didn't have transportation. He'd likely need to take her wherever she needed to go, whether that was the train station or to hire a car. He'd do it. Of course he would. But God, how was he going to get through it without falling to his knees and begging her to stay?

The same way he'd gotten through this morning. By reminding himself how much her life had been curtailed and run by someone else for way too fucking long. He had to do this because it was the right thing for her. Even if it meant cutting out his own heart. And that his dog would probably disown him.

The office door swung open, and Laura barged in. "Okay, out with it. You're in an absolute bear of a mood. What happened?"

"Nothing happened. I just have a headache."

"You've had headaches before and didnae go around scowling like you want to gut the customers. Where's Isobel?"

Fuck. Now his staff would know. They'd inevitably have opinions. But there was no getting around it. "Packing."

Laura's head kicked back. "Packing?"

"She's going back to her normal life. This was just a reprieve. A stopover. She was never going to stay."

Mouth agape, Laura's brows drew together. "Did she say that?"

"No, but you saw her last night. Music is what she's meant to do. She's meant to be out there. Touring, performing. There's nothing for her here. She doesn't want this tiny little life." And he'd never felt more insignificant in his.

Laura propped fisted hands on her generous hips. "Did you actually ask her that? Did she say that?"

"I didnae have to."

"So you're making assumptions."

"I'm doing what's right for her."

She made a low rumble of derision in the back of her throat. "You're being a right bampot."

Ewan glared. "I didnae ask for your opinion."

"Since when has that ever stopped me? You love that girl."

"That's no' the point."

"No' the point? No' the *point*? Ewan McBride, love is always the point. And if you havenae figured that out by now, you're worse off than I imagined."

"I dinna pay you for commentary on my life choices."

"Damned good thing, too, as you're making a total hash of it." On a huff, she flounced back out.

Fuck. She didn't know. Couldn't know what this was doing to him. When the door swung open again, he braced himself to tell his right hand exactly what she could do with her opinions.

But it was Hamish interrupting this time, his face set in uncharacteristic lines of temper. "What did you do?"

"What are you talking about?"

"Isobel called me to come pick her up, and she sounded upset. Given you two have been joined at the hip since the moment she got here, I ask again, what did you do?"

So he wasn't going to have to take her wherever she needed to go. It was what he'd wanted, but the confirmation of it offered him no relief. He rubbed at the ache in his temple. "Nothing."

"Then why the hell is she packing?"

He'd had about enough of people lambasting him for doing the right thing by her, so he didn't bother to curb the temper sizzling below the surface. "To go back to her real life. I always knew she'd have to once we resolved the threat. That's done.

She was never going to stay here working in my pub. Not when she's got all that talent bursting to be shared with the world. I'm just making it easier on her."

Hamish shook his head in disgust. "You're doing exactly what Burgette did."

That temper kicked up to a rolling boil. "What the fuck are you talking about?"

"You didn't ask her what she wants. You're just making the choice for her, taking away her options."

"I am not. I'm giving her all the options he denied her."

Hamish planted his hands on the desk and leaned in as if delivering an argument to a jury. "No, you're choosing some noble sacrifice and telling yourself it's in her best interest without actually having a real conversation. Without telling her the relevant detail that you're in love with her."

Ewan shoved up from his chair. "How can I say that? How can I use my feelings to manipulate her?"

"That's not manipulation, you dolt. That's communication. Which, apparently, you're absolute shite at."

"I dinna have to defend my decisions to you."

"No, you don't. And there's no defense you could make that would convince me you're being anything but completely and totally aff yer heid. But if this is your course, that's your choice. It's the wrong choice. But you do you. You always have. I'm getting out of here. Isobel's waiting."

On his way out, he slammed the door hard enough to rattle the pictures on the walls.

Ewan dropped back into his chair and scrubbed both hands over his stubbled cheeks. Was this what life was going to be like from now on? Everyone weighing in on his life, as if it was any of their bloody business? They weren't the ones living it.

But he couldn't deny that Hamish had gotten in his head. The last thing Ewan wanted was to be anything like that bawbag Burgette. He'd been utterly determined not to influence her one way or the other, so she could make an unbiased decision. He'd convinced himself that telling her how he felt would be an unfair weight on the side of asking her to stay. A part of him had assumed she knew. God knew, it seemed like everyone else did.

But what if she didn't realize? What if, in all his efforts to keep from influencing her, he'd actually withheld vital information? What if he'd actually made her think he didn't care at all? Hamish had said she'd sounded upset. She hadn't been upset when he'd left. Not that he'd been able to tell.

*But you didn't stick around, did you? And she's had lots of practice hiding her feelings.*

What if he'd gotten everything wrong?

Maybe he did owe her at least a conversation to clarify where he was coming from. Even if she still left, he didn't want her leaving, thinking their time together hadn't mattered to him.

## 18

Isobel wiped at the tears streaming down her cheeks. "Thank you for not asking."

Hamish glanced over from the driver's seat of his sensible sedan. "I figure you'll talk about it if you want to. Can I do anything to help?"

"You're doing it. Just drop me at the manor house at Lochmara. Charlotte's expecting me."

Isobel had no idea what she was doing, but Charlotte had been the go-to before when they'd been looking for somewhere she could stay. She'd find somewhere for Isobel to lay her head until she figured out what came next and figured out how to breathe again through the heartbreak.

Fifteen minutes later, he rolled to a stop in the circular drive in front of the house. They both climbed out.

Hamish gave her shoulder a brotherly squeeze. "Are you sure you want me to just leave you here?"

"For now." She shouldered her duffel bag. Well, technically Ciara's duffel bag. The one that contained everything she owned. The only thing remaining of the life she'd built here. Of the life she'd thought she'd continue to lead.

She supposed the rest of the things that had traveled with her on tour were... somewhere. Assuming Paul hadn't destroyed or tossed them. And there were the possessions at the penthouse apartment in New York that Paul had preferred during their rare downtime. But she wasn't up to going through whatever hoops would be necessary to track it down. Maybe she'd have Hamish do that, too. But later. No sense in wasting time on it yet.

The kitchen door opened, and Charlotte stepped out, dark gaze sweeping over her in an instant. "Oh, honey."

Moments later she was enfolded in a cinnamon-scented hug that had the tears cranking up again. Dimly, she was aware of Hamish reiterating that he was there if she needed him, then Charlotte was ushering her inside.

"You just sit yourself down right here with Kyla. I made snickerdoodles. Do you want some?"

"Okay." Isobel wilted into a chair.

Kyla immediately took her hand. "What's happened?"

From across the kitchen, Charlotte asked, "Is it something with your manager?"

"No, no. He's still in jail. Ewan kicked me out."

"What?" Their shrieks of astonishment echoed off the stone floor.

"I'm puttin' on the kettle for tea. Kyla, honey, get her some tissues."

For a few minutes, they just let her cry it out. Then Charlotte brought the tea to the table, along with a plate of still warm cookies.

"Okay, we're armed with warm beverages and sugar. Tell us what happened," Kyla insisted.

Isobel mopped her eyes and drank the tea—some herbal blend that actually complimented the cinnamon sugar cookies really nicely. And through it all, she explained what Ewan had said. And what he hadn't. By the end of her story, the room held a palpable disgust.

"Ugh! Why are men so stupid?" Charlotte demanded.

Kyla broke a cookie in half with more force than was necessary. "He's being an eejit. Anybody with eyes can see that he's in love with you."

"Clearly, he's not. I thought we were on the same page. But this morning he was all 'go get back to your normal life. There's nothing keeping you here.' How does he not understand that I don't want that life anymore? I wanted the one that we were building here. At least the one I thought we were building." Fresh tears spilled over, no doubt hydrated by the tea.

Charlotte shook her head. "This smacks of a man doing a thing for what he perceives to be a woman's own good, without actually consulting her about what she wants."

Temper finally broke through to numb some of the pain, and Isobel latched onto it. "I have had so fucking much of that in my life, and I am so over it. He doesn't have the right to make this decision for me."

"He absolutely doesn't," Kyla agreed.

"Why are you accepting what he's saying as law?" Charlotte asked. "You have every right to force him to actually talk about this. A relationship takes two people."

The anger felt so much better than the heartbreak. "You're absolutely right. I should go down to the pub and confront him. Make him have the hard conversation he's clearly trying to avoid." Then at least she'd have her say.

As she shoved to her feet, Charlotte grabbed keys. "I'll drive."

Kyla levered herself out of the chair. "Can I come? Because I really want to see this."

"Why the hell not? The more the merrier."

"I can call Sophie and Ciara. They'd be happy to show up as additional backup. Or emotional support. Whichever is needed."

"Do it." Head full of righteous indignation, Isobel yanked open the door to find Ewan standing on the stoop just about to knock. Riding on temper, she snarled, "What are you doing here?"

"I came to talk to you."

She didn't know how he'd known where to find her and didn't care. All she knew was that he'd hurt her, and he was here, and all that repressed temper was boiling over.

"Talk. Talk? Now you want to talk? No, you're going to listen." Stepping forward, she poked him in the chest. Pain sang up her finger from the contact, but she didn't let it slow her. "You, Ewan McBride, are a coward. You don't get to send me packing like some sort of inconvenience. That is not what I am. That is not who I am. Not after everything we've been to each other. You have no right to make any kind of decision about what I want in my career. Did you even bother to ask me what I want? No, you didn't. You made assumptions."

Because her finger felt like she was driving it against a brick wall, she switched to her palm and shoved. He fell back a step, one brow winging up.

"Well, I am done with men making assumptions and making decisions for my own good. I don't want to go back to my 'real life.' I want a normal life. And I have a normal life here. That is what I want. And I wanted you, before you decided to go stupid on me. If you don't want me, fine. That's a different matter. But if this is just some bullheaded, idiotic, male notion that you somehow know best, then you can take your opinion and shove it up your very fine arse."

Throughout her tirade, she thought she saw a glimmer of something that might have been amusement in his eyes. But that couldn't be right.

"Are you finished?"

She considered the question. "For the moment."

He nodded once. "I love you."

Those three little words took all the wind out of her sails and had the pieces of her heart taking desperate flight. "Then why the bloody hell did you send me away?"

"I didn't want to influence your decision about what to do next. I didn't want to do anything to manipulate you into staying. You're meant for something so much bigger than here."

"That's for me to decide. From here on out, no one gets to tell me what to do with my talent but me. It's been the thing used to cage me my entire life, and I'm done with that. For the first time in my life, I'm going to do what I want. And I want you. I want this. I want us."

His face twisted in pain. "So do I. But I dinna want you to give up your music because of me."

"I'm not giving up my music. My career is probably going to look different moving forward. But I want it to be different. I'm tired of being on the road all the time. I'm tired of touring. I'm tired of all these massive concerts. I'm tired of other people having all the control. I want to take time to make music. I want to take time to live my life. I want to do it here with you."

An uncharacteristic vulnerability shone in his eyes. "Truly?"

"I love you, too. How did you not know that?"

"Oh, thank God." And at last he lost the stiffness and distance, his whole body relaxing as he reached for her.

She went willingly, wrapping him tight, even as she still kind of wanted to smack him. "Stubborn, foolish, wonderful man."

He pressed his cheek against her temple, holding her close to a heart that was pounding. "I'm sorry for being an eejit. For not actually asking what you wanted. I thought I was giving you choices, and I accidentally cut them off instead."

"Well, that was stupid."

A laugh rumbled in his chest. "Aye. I was told exactly that by multiple people."

"Then don't be stupid again."

"Oh, I'm sure if you stick around, I'll manage to screw up again. But I'll keep trying. For you, I'll always keep trying."

A throat cleared behind them. Charlotte. "So I'm guessing this means you aren't gonna need a cottage for the foreseeable future?"

Isobel looked up at him, arching a brow. "Do I?"

Ewan tightened his hold. "Only if you want one. I'd really like it if you'd come home."

*Home.* The thing she'd been looking for her whole life and had unexpectedly found with him.

"No, Charlotte. I won't be needing a cottage."

"That's good, because I already put your bag in Ewan's Land Rover."

"WE'RE GOING TO BE LATE!"

Ewan felt his lips twitch and wondered if Isobel would always be so enthusiastic about family dinners. "It's a come as you are when you can situation. There's no reason to rush."

She balled both hands on her hips and sent him a glare. "There wouldn't have been a reason to rush if you hadn't lured me into bed, thus necessitating a shower, where you also slowed down the whole process of making myself presentable."

The twitch turned into a full-on self-satisfied smirk. "I dinna recall you complaining. In fact, I'm reasonably sure I remember a lot of 'Yes, Ewan!' and 'More, Ewan!'"

Two flags of color bloomed in her fair cheeks. "Don't think I won't be exacting retribution later."

"Promises, promises." He only laughed when she thumped him on the arm.

He could humor her and pick up the pace to get on to Ardinmuir, but he really did want to give her the gift he'd gotten her. It was what he'd intended to do when he'd cornered her earlier, and then gotten sidetracked in magnificent fashion.

"Five more minutes. I've got something I want to give you."

When he reached to snag her around the waist, she danced out of reach, hiding behind Havoc's wagging bulk. "Oh, no. I know exactly what five more minutes means with you, and it's never *just* five more minutes."

"Again... dinna remember complaints. But no. That's no' what I meant. I got you something." He strode into the bedroom and retrieved the gift bag.

"A present?" Her eyes brightened with pleasure. "What is it?"

"Open it and see."

She tugged out the tissue paper and reached for what was wrapped inside. There was a faint metallic clink as she unwrapped the tissue paper around the wind chimes she'd admired that day at the Glenlaig Visitor's Center.

"Oh!" She lifted the chimes up and set the center string to swaying. The clear tones rang out, filling the room, and she closed her eyes to soak it in as she always seemed to do with any sort of music, as if shutting off her sight would more keenly enhance her hearing.

"I had Jeanne set them back for me that day we went shopping in the village."

Surprise and delight lit up her face. "You did?"

"I ken you wanted them and were trying to be practical and sensible. I meant to pick them up sooner, but with everything that happened, time got away from me. I thought maybe they'd remind you of home. Remind you that this is your home. Not just by circumstance or temporarily because it's safest. But because it's *yours*. Because I'm yours."

Those prismatic eyes shimmered. She gently laid the wind chimes on the table and crossed to him, reaching up to frame his face. "Damn you for your immeasurable sweetness when we're already late." Her lips brushed his in a slow, sensual promise. "I love them. And I love you. And I'll show you exactly how much later, but we are not showing up a conspicuous hour late with sex hair."

He gripped her hips, pulled her against the fresh erection. "That's fine. There's something to be said for anticipation."

She was the one who rubbed against him, her eyes drooping as a little whimpering moan sounded at the back of her throat. He thought her resolve might crack, but she stepped back with a quick shake of her head. "Later." Another glance at his crotch. "Definitely later."

She picked up the bread she'd made and held it in front of her like a shield. "Let's go."

Twenty minutes later, they were stepping into the big stone kitchen at Ardinmuir, where the last of the dishes were being set on the table.

"Perfect timing!" The twinkle in Angus's eye suggested he knew exactly why they'd been late. "What's that you have there, Isobel?"

"A cottage loaf. I followed your recipe to the letter."

"It's a fine-looking loaf. Here now. We'll slice it and add it to a basket."

When they'd settled around the table and everyone had been served, Ewan cleared his throat. "We've got an announcement to make."

Across the table, Ciara's eyes lit and she bit her lip, dancing a little in her chair.

Charlotte pumped her fist. "Called it!"

Ewan arched a brow. "You dinna even ken what the news is."

She just grinned. "I can guess."

Kyla flashed an amused smile in her direction. "I think perhaps you're getting a wee bit ahead of things. What's the news?"

Isobel picked up the thread. "I've been in contact with my record label."

Ciara's face fell. "That was definitely not what I thought the news was."

Yeah, Ewan knew what she and Charlotte had been expecting.

"I'm contractually obligated to finish my tour. We're currently still negotiating about the performances I missed, but considering the fact that Paul's kidnapping attempt has finally hit the media, they're being a lot more reasonable about that than they might otherwise."

There'd been a small swarm of reporters who'd shown up in town, wanting to land an interview with Elizabeth Duncan. Isobel had handled the whole thing like the professional she was, but Ewan had hated every minute and spent most of the time standing in a corner, glowering as she'd spoken to them.

"So what's the plan?" Sophie asked.

"I have to be in Barcelona on Friday to resume. There are two months of the original tour left, and they're working on scheduling out makeup performances, which will probably stretch out another couple of months past that."

The expressions that had initially been so hopeful suddenly turned concerned as they all looked at Ewan while trying to appear like they weren't.

"So you're leaving?" Connor asked at last.

"For a bit, yes. Besides the tour, there are a lot of details I need to sort out, and I can't do most of that here."

Ewan stretched an arm along the back of her chair. "Which brings us to the news: I'm going with her."

"Ewan's my new head of security and personal bodyguard. After what happened with Paul, the team the label hired was fired, so he's bringing on a couple of his friends to fill out the roster."

"Patterson and Conroy. You've heard me mention them before."

"We're supposed to meet up with them in Barcelona, and they'll go along on the remainder of the tour as well. I confess, I'm looking forward to meeting Finley and Alex."

Ciara made a choking noise.

Raleigh helpfully thumped her on the back. "You okay, there?"

"Yeah, yeah. My water just went down the wrong pipe. Alex Conroy is his name?"

Ewan frowned at her. "Aye, why?"

She shook her head. "No reason. I've never heard you call him anything but Conroy. I think I imagined his first name was something ridiculous, like Leopold or Barnaby."

He shook his head. "You are so weird."

Ciara crossed her eyes and stuck her tongue out, as she'd been doing since she was wee. "Do you need me to keep Havoc again?"

Ewan resisted the urge to stick his tongue out in return. "He's actually going with us."

"On the road?" Malcolm asked.

Isobel flashed a smile. "Well, one of the perks of being the talent is that I can make outrageous requests. I never have before, but I figured bringing our hundred-and-thirty pound dog with us was a good place to start. If I say he's my emotional support animal, they aren't going to argue. Especially after everything I went through. Which also means they have to give me a kinder schedule, so win-win all around."

"What will you do about the pub?" Connor asked. "I can help out, if need be."

"Appreciated, Cousin, but I'm doing what I should've done in the first place and making Laura my partner. The Stag's Head is as much hers as mine. So she's going to take over more of the running of things, which—let's be honest—she already did. That'll leave me free to travel with Isobel, as needed, for whatever she wants to do."

"And what is it you want to do, lass?" Munro asked.

"Well, as I said, lots of details to sort out. Paul's trial will be coming up."

"That's as close to a slam dunk as you can expect legally," Hamish put in. "There's no fighting the kidnapping charge, and I suspect he'll be facing additional charges before it's over. He'll be going away for a good long while."

"Thank God for that. I've been receiving queries from various and sundry prospective agents. I'm letting those ride for now because, essentially, once this tour obligation is over, I'm taking a sabbatical. I want to rerecord my albums, work on new music. And otherwise, I plan to settle in at home and just enjoy small town life. In theory, by the time the tour is over, things should have settled down in the village, so we can all get back to normal."

"So, you're going to stay?" Ciara asked.

Isobel looked up at him and smiled. "Aye, I'm going to stay."

And that would always be Ewan's personal miracle because he never would've imagined that she'd choose him over the life she'd led. But they were both making room and rebuilding their careers in a way that meant they could be together. It might've been unconventional, but it would work for them. Because what that storm had brought together, nothing could put asunder.

# EPILOGUE

"I can't believe it's over!"

Isobel staggered a bit as drummer Maria Cuellar threw her arms around her, still a little drunk from last night's end-of-tour celebration. Surrounded by luggage, they stood in the lobby of the same hotel where Isobel had played with a little boy for fun all those months ago.

Beside them, Ukranian cellist Yelena Marchenko propped her fist on one cocked hip. "I can't believe we've been touring with you all this time and we had no *idea* you were a karaoke goddess."

Isobel laughed. "To be fair, I didn't know that either. I'd never done karaoke. And I'm reasonably sure the only reason you got me up there was the margaritas."

"Doesn't change the fact that you absolutely slayed. And we're gonna miss you like crazy."

Isobel found great satisfaction in ending the tour in London, the city where she'd found the courage to change things. Everything about the past several months had been different. Without Paul around to interfere, she'd been able to actually connect with everyone she'd toured with. She'd been terrified to go back, worried they'd be angry at her disappearing act. But everybody had been so understanding and gracious. There'd been multiple stories that had come out about all the other things Paul had done, so when he'd been convicted a few weeks ago, there'd been celebration among everyone on the tour. The entire tone was lighter and so much more fun. Isobel still intended to take a significant break from touring, but she wasn't as completely against the idea as she had been. For now, she was looking forward to getting down to rerecording her first album and was excited to have multiple talented musicians enthusiastically joining her for the process.

"It'll only be a few weeks before we meet up to record in Glasgow. We all deserve a break."

Maria's deep brown eyes sparkled. "Admit it. You just want time alone at the beach with that sexy hunk of a bodyguard."

Not that he hadn't been with her every day and night during the tour, but she wasn't wrong. Isobel blushed and shrugged. "I mean…"

Yelena looked over to where Ewan stood a little apart with Alex and Finley and hummed in appreciation. "They do grow them well in Scotland. I can't say I minded the change in security staff at all."

"No, indeed," Maria concurred. "And we're going to miss this big fluffy hunk of love." She scruffed Havoc's ears, sending the big dog to his back in groaning, leg-wheeling ecstasy.

Yelena crouched to rub his belly. "Who's a good boy? You're a good boy. I request we always have a tour dog."

"I feel like we can make that happen."

With one more round of hugs for both her and the dog, her friends—her *friends*—headed out to catch their respective flights home.

Feeling buoyant and relieved, she went to join the guys.

"Gentlemen. I believe we can officially call this tour finished. I thank you so much for being here."

Finley grinned at her and jerked a thumb in Ewan's direction. "I wouldnae have missed seeing this one sloppy in love for anything in the world."

Ewan calmly flipped him off.

"Ach, he's just jealous," Alex insisted. "Seriously though, it's been a pleasure, and we're glad we could help."

Isobel hugged them both. "You'll have to come up to Glenlaig to visit us."

"That'll have to wait. Quinn's finally out." The grim set to Alex's jaw suggested that might not have been of Callum's own choosing. "Finn and I are heading out to meet him shortly."

Knowing how much Ewan worried about his friend, she turned into him. "Do you want to go with them? Our beach trip can wait."

"He willnae be ready for all of us yet. There will be plenty of time. Besides, we're due back in town for Connor and Sophie's wedding right after our vacation." Ewan shifted his gaze back to his friends. "But you'll keep me updated, aye?"

Finley nodded. "Aye."

Something had caught Alex's attention behind her. Curious, she turned as he muttered, "Oh, shite."

"Miss Duncan?"

Putting on her for-the-fans smile, Isobel nodded at the woman, whom she pegged to be in her mid to late forties. She was a little pale, and her hands trembled.

"Hello, I... I'm so sorry to bother you."

In the months since she'd gone back on tour, Isobel had been able to indulge her desire to interact with fans as much as she wanted. The outpouring of support from her fanbase had been humbling, and she wanted to do anything she could to thank them. Wanting to put the woman more at ease, she stepped away from Ewan. "It's no bother at all. How can I help you?" She could certainly take a minute to chat and give an autograph or take a selfie.

The woman linked her hands together. "I just... I wanted to say that your music is so awe-inspiring. You're so incredibly talented."

"Thank you! That's so kind. Do you have a favorite piece?"

The corners of her mouth curved a little. "It's not one of yours but, Saint-Saëns' 'The Swan.'"

Something about that half smile seemed vaguely familiar. "Oh, that's absolutely one of my favorites. My father used to play it for me."

"Padrig used to play it for hours when we were young."

Isobel froze, her mouth going dry. "Excuse me?"

"He sweet-talked me into playing the piano part, but I didnae have the aptitude he did."

"Who are you?" The question barely came out stronger than a whisper.

"Aislinn Donnchadh. Well, Lindsay now. But my brother was Padrig Donnchadh." She offered a hopeful smile. "I'm your aunt. It's so very nice to meet you, Isobel."

Too stunned to speak, she could only stare.

Aislinn rushed on. "I have no idea what Padrig told you about the family. Harsh things were said on both sides before he left, but our parents always regretted it. They never saw him again. We, none of us, knew about you until I saw a video of your concert in Glenlaig and heard your name. I knew you had to be his child."

Isobel could feel Ewan at her back and knew that one glance from her would have him intervening. But she kept her focus on Aislinn. Her aunt. She could see it now. The shape of her father's eyes. Her eyes. And something about the line of Aislinn's jaw.

Tears welled in Aislinn's eyes. "We didnae ken Padrig had died until... well, until recently. And your mother... I'm so, so sorry. We should've... well. We should've done a lot of things." She knuckled the tears away and squared her shoulders. "Look,

I have no expectations. I ken I'm a stranger to you and that you may want nothing to do with any of us after the way our parents treated Padrig and your mother. I just wanted to give you an open invitation to speak with me, in case you had any questions or just... anything. The family would love the chance to get to know you."

"Family?" Isobel echoed.

"You have me and another uncle and several cousins. Even some second cousins. We're all up mostly around Portlethen, south of Aberdeen."

Isobel had no idea what to do with that.

Aislinn pressed a paper into her hand. "This is my contact information. Email, phone, address. I'll understand if you dinna care to use it, but I hope you will. Someday."

Then she melted away and strode out of the hotel.

Isobel didn't move. She had actual blood family. In some dim, distant part of her brain, it had occurred to her to wonder from time to time whether any of her father's kin were still around, but she'd never thought to track them down. They hadn't welcomed her mother, so why would they welcome her? And why would she want to get to know people who'd cut her father off merely for loving the wrong person? But Aislinn hadn't seemed cold or hateful. She'd seemed... kind.

Ewan's arms slipped around her, and he pressed his lips to her temple. "Are you okay, love?"

"Is this real?"

"Aye." When he hesitated, she looked up at him. "I had Alex dig into your family at the start of the tour. Once your real name came out publicly, I figured if there was someone left, they'd come out of the woodwork. I wanted to have some idea whether that might be a legitimate desire to reconnect or if they'd be money seekers."

"Oh."

"Your grandparents are no longer living, and the others

seem stable and happy, and dinna have any reason to seek you out other than exactly what she said."

"There's a dossier if you want it," Alex added.

"Of course there is," Isobel muttered. But there was no heat in it. These men had been tasked to protect her. She wasn't going to quibble about their methods.

"I was planning to tell you about it when we got home. I didnae anticipate she'd come to you."

She had family who'd sought her out. Had they tried before and been unable to do so because of the name change? Or because Paul had prevented it somehow?

"I have no idea how I feel about this."

"You can leave all of it," Ewan reminded her. "You have family back in Glenlaig. This doesnae change that. Or you can take the time to meet them. Either way, you've got a week away to process and think about it. There's no timeline on making a decision."

"I think... I need to meet them. It might not go further than that, but I think it might give me some closure."

His arms tightened around her. "Then we'll do that."

"You'll come with me?"

"Anywhere, always."

There was no greater reassurance he could offer. With her fierce Highland protector by her side, she could face anything.

HAMISH WATCHED Connor square his shoulders in front of the full-length mirror. He looked a little pale against the dark blue of his Argyll jacket.

"Are you nervous?"

"To marry Sophie? No. I canna wait to start the rest of my life with the woman of my dreams. A little afraid she'll wake up one day and think she's made a huge mistake? Maybe."

Hamish clapped him on the shoulder. "Never gonna happen. She adores you."

"God, I hope so. I've been waiting all my life for her." Connor turned, gripping Hamish's shoulder, so they mirrored each other. His blue eyes were serious. "Thank you for everything you did to get me out of that marriage pact so that I can be here today."

"Of course."

But a frisson of guilt ran through Hamish. He'd only partly done it for his best friend. In truth, he'd largely done it for Afton. He'd wanted to make things better for her. And now that his marriage was completely over, he could acknowledge to himself that he'd done it a little for himself, too. For all the good that had done him. No one had heard a word from her since she'd left eighteen months before.

He wondered where she was. What she'd been doing. If she was happy. If she was safe.

In truth, he spent far too much time worrying and wondering about all of that, when he had so many other things to tend to. Like raising his daughter and making up for her mother's apparent abdication of parenthood. Building his law practice. Renovating the two-hundred-year-old farmhouse he'd been daft enough to buy. And today, standing up beside his best friend to watch him marry the woman he loved.

No matter his personal motives, it was worth so much to Hamish to be here for that. Because he knew what it was to Connor to have the freedom to choose love over duty.

Angus appeared in the doorway. "It's time. Are you ready, lad?"

Connor beamed. "Abso-fucking-lutely."

They made their way through the halls of the old stone church. Connor and Sophie had considered getting married at Ardinmuir, but in the end, they'd elected to follow MacKean family tradition and tie the knot at the village kirk. Ewan joined the three of them as they stepped out into the sanctuary. Angus peeled off to meet the bride, as he was walking her down the aisle, and the rest of them took their places in front, Hamish noted that the room was packed. It felt as if everyone in the village was here, stuffed in like sausages on the wooden pews. In the corners, video cameras were set up to stream the ceremony to others who didn't fit inside. Sophie had drawn the line at having anyone stand through the wedding.

Raleigh sat with Munro, Charlotte, Malcolm, and Gavin in the front row. Baby Lily was tucked into his arms, miraculously napping through the murmur of voices. Ciara and the rest of the McBrides were right behind. There'd been no formal bride-and groom-side seating, as Sophie and Connor were friends with everyone. Freya sat with her grandparents a few rows back, bouncing in her seat in the pretty green velvet dress she'd worn for the occasion. She waved at him, and Hamish wiggled his fingers back with a smile.

At some silent signal, Isobel began to play the processional, the strains of her violin filling the chamber with joy. The doors at the back opened and Swayze Parish stepped inside, grin bright as she made the journey down to the front. As matron of honor, Kyla was next, her long red hair twisted up in some fancy arrangement with jeweled pins that matched the vibrant red bridesmaid dresses. As Freya had outgrown flower girl status, they'd skipped that, and foregone the ring bearer too. Hamish had Sophie's wedding ring in his coat pocket, and Kyla was carrying Connor's. She took her place opposite Hamish, and they all turned to face the rear as the music shifted once more.

Sophie seemed to float down the aisle, resplendent in a blue sari with red and gold accents that echoed Connor's tartan. She was radiant, beaming with a joy that warmed Hamish's heart.

He thought of his own wedding to Dayna, held in a posh

hotel in Edinburgh, per her request. It had been small, exclusive, and expensive, with none of the love and tradition that had gone into this one. And he definitely hadn't been looking at his bride the way Connor was looking at Sophie right now.

How could he have deluded himself so thoroughly that he'd been in love? Maybe some part of him had believed he could make it so through sheer force of will. It hadn't been all bad. They'd enjoyed each other for a long time. As long as he'd been willing to submit to staying in Edinburgh, mingling in the social circles she preferred. But it hadn't been home. It had never been home. And over the years, the strain had begun to fray whatever connection they'd had to start.

Sophie reached the front, taking Connor's hand with a look of love so bright Hamish had to avert his gaze for a moment.

He hadn't had that. Not ever. The realization made him ache.

Really, it was best for everyone that Dayna had had the affair. That they were over. If Hamish wasn't exactly happy, he was content with the life he was building here with his daughter, surrounded by friends and family.

"Dearly beloved—"

As the minister welcomed the guests, Hamish tried to turn his attention to the ceremony. But he didn't really hear much of the introduction. Not until the end of the remarks.

"If anyone here knows of any lawful impediment to the marriage of Sophie and Connor, speak now or forever hold your peace."

The heavy wooden door at the back of the sanctuary creaked open. As one, everyone in the church turned to look at the latecomer.

In shock, Hamish's hand shot out to clamp on Connor's shoulder, more because his own legs felt unsteady at the sight of the apparition. Her pale blonde hair was loose around her shoulders, and fresh snow dusted the navy wool of her coat.

Even from this distance, Hamish would swear her hazel eyes were trained directly on him.

Afton Lennox had finally come home.

### Choose Your Next Romance

SQUEE! I know you've been waiting for Afton and Hamish way back since *Jilting The Kilt,* and I am SO EXCITED to bring you their story. *Single Dad in a Kilt* is now available!

Meanwhile, if you'd like to see a little bit more of Isobel and Ewan's happily ever after, you can grab their bonus epilogue here: https://books.bookfunnel.com/a-little-lagniappe/ ah72q5seln

Want some more woman-in-trouble, forced proximity protector romance? Have you checked out my Bad Boy Bakers series? It begins with a twofer because Book 1, *Mixed Up With a Marine,* is a second chance romance—Brax thinks they're divorced; Mia knows they're not. This one's full of secrets and band of brothers goodness. You can nab the prequel, *Rescued By a Bad Boy,* to see how Mia and Brax went from friends to lovers.

# OTHER BOOKS BY KAIT NOLAN

A complete and up-to-date list of all my books can be found at https://kaitnolan.com.

- *Wrapped Up with a Ranger* (Holt and Cayla)
- *Stirred Up by a SEAL* (Jonah and Rachel)
- *Hung Up on the Hacker* (Cash and Hadley)
- *Caught Up with the Captain* (Grey and Rebecca)

### RESCUE MY HEART SERIES
### SMALL TOWN MILITARY ROMANCE

- *Someone Like You* (Ivy and Harrison)
- *What I Like About You* (Laurel and Sebastian)
- *Bad Case of Loving You* (Paisley and Ty prequel)
  Included in *Made For Loving You* (Paisley and Ty)

### THE MISFIT INN SERIES
### SMALL TOWN FAMILY ROMANCE

- *When You Got A Good Thing* (Kennedy and Xander)
- *Til There Was You* (Misty and Denver)
- *Those Sweet Words* (Pru and Flynn)
- *Stay A Little Longer* (Athena and Logan)
- *Bring It On Home* (Maggie and Porter)
- *Come Away with Me* (Moses and Zuri)

### MEN OF THE MISFIT INN
### SMALL TOWN SOUTHERN ROMANCE

- *Let It Be Me* (Emerson and Caleb)
- *Our Kind of Love* (Abbey and Kyle)
- *Don't You Wanna Stay* (Deanna and Wyatt)
- *Until We Meet Again* (Samantha and Griffin prequel)
- *Come A Little Closer* (Samantha and Griffin)
- *Just Wanted You To Know* (Livia and Declan)

### WISHFUL ROMANCE SERIES

## SMALL TOWN SOUTHERN ROMANCE

- *Once Upon A Coffee* (Avery and Dillon)
- *To Get Me To You* (Cam and Norah)
- *Know Me Well* (Liam and Riley)
- *Be Careful, It's My Heart* (Brody and Tyler)
- *Just For This Moment* (Myles and Piper)
- *Wish I Might* (Reed and Cecily)
- *Turn My World Around* (Tucker and Corinne)
- *Dance Me A Dream* (Jace and Tara)
- *See You Again* (Trey and Sandy)
- *The Christmas Fountain* (Chad and Mary Alice)
- *You Were Meant For Me* (Mitch and Tess)
- *A Lot Like Christmas* (Ryan and Hannah)
- *Dancing Away With My Heart* (Zach and Lexi)

## WISHING FOR A HERO SERIES (A WISHFUL SPINOFF SERIES)
### SMALL TOWN ROMANTIC SUSPENSE

- *Make You Feel My Love* (Judd and Autumn)
- *Watch Over Me* (Nash and Rowan)
- *Can't Take My Eyes Off You* (Ethan and Miranda)
- *Burn For You* (Sean and Delaney)

## MEET CUTE ROMANCE
### SMALL TOWN SHORT ROMANCE

- *Once Upon A Snow Day*
- *Once Upon A New Year's Eve*
- *Once Upon An Heirloom*
- *Once Upon A Coffee*
- *Once Upon A Campfire*
- *Once Upon A Rescue*

### SUMMER CAMP
### CONTEMPORARY ROMANCE

- *Once Upon A Campfire*
- *Second Chance Summer*

# ABOUT KAIT

Kait is a Mississippi native, who often swears like a sailor, calls everyone sugar, honey, or darlin', and can wield a bless your heart like a saber or a Snuggie, depending on requirements.

You can find more information on this *USA Today* best selling and RITA ® Award-winning author and her books on her website http://kaitnolan.com.

Do you need more small town sass and spark? Sign up for <u>her newsletter</u> to hear about new releases, book deals, and exclusive content!